CAMPUS NIGHT LIFE

Daisy dashed to the door of the little brick office anchoring the greenhouse. "It's locked!" She clopped around back, into the specimen camellias, and yelled at the window. "Leo?"

No answer. She scurried back to watch the security guard try one key, then another, until he found one that turned in the lock.

Daisy pushed first through the door, running past the long black counters, around the corner to Leo's glassed-in office. She screamed like a woman on fire.

Teddy reached the corner half a second later. Bloody handprints raked the office glass. Daisy had sunk to her knees. Teddy dashed in and clutched the doorframe.

On the floor Leo lay on his belly, the back of his blue oxford shirt embellished with blooming stab wounds.

Other Professor Teodora Morelli Mysteries by
Linda French
from Avon Twilight

TALKING RAIN

Switching off the stuffing machine, Teddy said, "It's Leo, isn't it?" The Saturday overtime seamstresses looked up from their work.

Mortified, Teddy dragged her sister into the office and closed the door. Throwing last spring's Marigold Rabbit out of the visitor's chair, Teddy pushed Daisy down and pumped a cup of coffee from the vacuum pot. Handing it to Daisy, she said, "You have to tell somebody what's wrong."

"Nothing." Daisy ignored the coffee. "I can't tell you."

"I'm not going to tell Marmee."

"You can't anyway, she's in the Galapagos by now." Daisy quavered, her face wracked with pain. "Are you going to water her plants, or should I?"

"Don't change the subject." Teddy moved in close. "I didn't tell Marmee when Leo bought the Mercedes." Teddy stroked Daisy's hair. "You've got to tell somebody, *cara*."

At the sound of their mother's own endearment, Daisy began bawling. She wailed loudly once, then quieted so the seamstresses wouldn't stop their machines. Plucking a tissue from the white wicker box, Daisy blew her nose. "One of my seamstresses quit."

Teddy narrowed her eyes and waited: seamstresses quit as regularly as Pacific fronts.

Then she blurted, "Leo has a mistress."

Teddy gasped. "Daisy! That's impossible. Leo adores you." She offered the tissue box again. "You don't really believe that, do you?"

"Teddy, she's even younger than you, and she's a *real* artist. She draws women with saggy breasts and dead houseplants." Daisy gestured to the sunny watercolors of Kris, and Velvet, and Raphael from the experimental line of angel bunnies. "I can't compete with that."

"Compete?" Brushing back Daisy's hair, Teddy regarded her sister's face, a familiar variation on the Morelli theme: wavy brown hair, Marmee's porcelain skin, and in Daisy's

1

From the balcony, Teddy Morelli dumped a forty-pound bale of fiberfill over the rail. She stared into the hopper, mesmerized as the compressed air of the stuffing machine ravaged the bale, plumping it to thirty times its former volume. A single block of fiberfill would fatten seventy-five of her sister Daisy's exquisite woolen bunnies. But down on the floor of Bunny Business, Inc., her sister was not happy.

Daisy sat forlornly at the stuffing machine—a wildly specialized piece of late-forties equipment she had picked up in Los Angeles. Holding a limp Kris Kringle Bunny over the fill pipe, she pressed the foot pedal twice, plumping Kris's skinny two-hundred-dollar leg. Sliding the pipe out, she repeated the process on the rest of his droopy limbs.

This was going to be *the* big year for Bunny Business. Nordstrom's was using bunnies in its Christmas displays and had ordered forty-five magnum-sized Kringles and sixty-five hero-sized Velvets. Velvet wore a black Irish cloak lined with pink satin. She was the seamstresses' favorite.

Teddy trotted down the iron steps and sat by her big sister. Daisy was clamped into protective earphones and glanced up like a lost fairy child.

Teddy mouthed, "What's the matter?"

Daisy shook her head. Never mind. Tears welled in her eyes.

An invention of Satan? Why this Satan's drink is so delicious, it would be a pity to let the Infidels have exclusive use of it. We shall fool Satan by baptizing it and making it a truly Christian beverage.

Pope Clement VII (1475–1534)
on tasting his first cup of coffee

To Paulie, Rick, Mary, Joanie,
Joe, and Madeline,
but not necessarily in that order

AVON BOOKS, INC.
1350 Avenue of the Americas
New York, New York 10019

Copyright © 1998 by Linda French
Published by arrangement with the author
Visit our website at **http://www.AvonBooks.com/Twilight**
Library of Congress Catalog Card Number: 98-93179
ISBN: 0-380-79575-2

First Avon Twilight Printing: December 1998

AVON TWILIGHT TRADEMARK REG. U.S. PAT. OFF. AND IN OTHER COUN-TRIES, MARCA REGISTRADA, HECHO EN U.S.A.

Printed in the U.S.A.

WCD 10 9 8 7 6 5 4 3 2

Coffee To Die For

A PROFESSOR TEODORA MORELLI MYSTERY

LINDA FRENCH

case, impossibly beautiful liquid almond eyes. "She can't be as pretty as you."

Daisy shook her head. "She's got red hair and she's really, really *cute*. Her name's even cute: Molly Thistle."

Teddy screwed up her face. "Daisy, that sounds like one of your bunnies."

"I know," Daisy wailed. "Spring line."

"But, Daisy." Teddy rubbed her sister's back. "You don't know they're sleeping together. Maybe he just has a crush on her, and he's embarrassed."

"You don't understand." Daisy blew her nose. "I found a rolled-up portrait she did of him in his office, he wasn't even going to show me, he acted like it wasn't important. It's really good, Teddy—she did it from the side. She even likes his hairy ears."

Teddy bit her lip.

Daisy heaved. "I just wish he never would have *started* on coffee DNA. We were so much happier when he was doing cauliflower mold for State Extension." She balled up the Kleenex and made an easy two points into the antique French waste can.

"Daisy, you don't mean that. You said yourself that being funded by AgroGene was like being funded by God. Anyway, you'll be proud of him tonight at the coffee cupping." Teddy dropped onto the pickled-pine bench. "You know what? I bet Leo and Molly Thistle are just friends, and you're just stressed out and imagining all this."

Daisy stood and dabbed at her eyes. "Teddy, I can't do this right now, we're too behind on the Kringles. And Mungo wants to see me on his break."

"Mungo!" Teddy leaped up and grabbed her coat. "Mungo makes me feel like a dolt." Mungo was Daisy's cutter, the man who made sure every Italian inch of velvet-flocked mohair was put to good use. He was also a Civil War buff.

"No, Teddy, stay." Daisy put out a dainty manicured hand. "Mungo likes you."

"What he likes is to make me feel like an idiot." Teddy fidgeted. "How am I suppose to know where General Sherman slept in Savannah?" The phone rang and Daisy punched the speakerphone. "Bunny Business, Daisy Faber speaking. How may I help you?" Automatically she began opening mail with her hands.

"Big D, is Teddy there?" It was Aurie Scholl, the orthopedic surgeon who had dropped Teddy five years ago to marry a cheerleader, and now, divorced, had recently decided he was interested again.

Teddy exhaled. "I'm right here, Aurie."

"Hey, we on for tonight?"

"Can't. Prior obligations." His own words for the last four weekends.

"Rats. I just dropped the Governor's Task Force so I wouldn't have to go to their cocktail party tonight."

Teddy rolled her eyes. "Go back, Aurie. The governor needs you."

"But isn't tonight Leo's pow-wow with the secret coffee?"

"That's right. So maybe we can get together later in the week. I'll be here in Seattle for most of spring break."

"But I thought the table over at Oliveri Coffee Company was really big." He let it hang there and Daisy finally answered, "You're entirely welcome to join us tonight, Aurie. The cupping starts at eight."

"Outstanding! Thank you, Daisy. Put Stubby back on, will you?"

"I'm right here, Aurie." Teddy straightened her spine to make the most of her five feet, three inches.

"Why don't I pick you up at seven-thirty and we can go over together?"

"Fine, Aurie. See you then."

"Great. And could you wear your little black femur skirt, and that fuzzy little sweater?"

"Aurie, listen." Teddy sighed. "You've got to give me some space here, okay?"

"*Liebchen*! Of course! Solar systems. Galaxies." He hung up the phone.

Teddy fumed. "Daisy, why did you let h—"

There was a knock on the door and Teddy opened it to a scrawny chinless man in an Atlanta baseball cap. He wore slim-cut jeans and cowboy boots, and smelled of cigarettes—or autumn bonfires, although it was the end of March.

"Mungo, how ya doing?" asked Teddy.

"Fair to middling." Mungo was from Calhoun, Georgia, and sounded as if he had taken elocution from Minnie Pearl. "And yourself, Miss Teddy? How's the history business?"

Teddy shrugged. "They keep making it, we'll keep dishing it out."

"Why you down in Seattle?"

"Spring break. But I have to go back to Bellingham late tonight and grade."

"Dandy." He settled into the visitor's chair, hauling up a black-tooled boot for all to admire. "Say, I found that book on Vicksburg you were talking about, it's way wrong—it's worse than Ken Burns."

Teddy flinched. "Really?"

"Oh, yeah. That book says the Yankees defeated General Bowen in early skirmishes at Port Gibson, but I know for a fact Bowen was staging a *strategic retreat* so that he could fight more effectively in the later critical campaign for the city."

Teddy crossed her arms. "Is that so?"

"Everybody knows that. Also your book says that during the siege of Vicksburg people were eating rats, but I talked to a guy lives there says rats was just a Yankee rumor, got started when the Episcopal soup kitchen served up squirrel meat—squirrel just happens to *look* like rat when you skin it."

"I didn't know that."

Mungo snorted. "Oh, yeah. That book's full of errors, I been highlighting 'em with marker. You want to take a gander after I've finished?"

Teddy scratched a tear duct. "I think I'll take a pass on that, Mungo. I can barely keep up with Pacific Northwest. Which reminds me . . ." She made cheery eye contact. "Could you tell Peg I brought those brochures about San Juan Island? You guys taking a vacation or something?"

Mungo's eyes suddenly glazed blue cold. "I guess you haven't heard."

"Heard what?"

"Peg and I are getting a divorce. I moved out last week."

"Oh, Mungo, I'm so sorry."

Mungo snarled. "Shoulda just left her at the truckstop in Memphis. I'd be playing professional baseball now if it weren't for her. You do know I was talking to the Atlanta 'A' league right before I left, don't you?"

Teddy recited, before he could: "Piedmont Muni M.V.P., three years in a row."

"Humongous truckstop right across the river in Memphis. I walked past the diesel pumps and this voice calls out, clear as day: 'Leave her and go West, young man.'" Mungo grabbed the toe of his boot. "That was God talking."

"I can imagine."

"I wasn't *cut out* to be a materials expert." He waited for his joke. "As I told Miss Daisy, I'm only helping her temporarily because I used to cut raincoats back in Calhoun for London Fog—it's a very prestigious company."

"I know that, Mungo."

Mungo glanced quickly at Daisy's puffy eyes, then decided his own problem carried more weight. "Miss Daisy, I know people should try to keep their personal problems off the shop floor, but I'm having trouble concentrating, and I thought I better tell you before I cut into the alpaca."

Daisy gasped. "Yes, Mungo, what is it? We're all family here."

"Thank you, Miss Daisy, I appreciate that." Mungo nestled comfortably into the chintz pillows. "Yesterday I unpacked at my new digs and I found I was missing a rare and valuable hubcap from my collection. It's a 1962 piece from a California after-market company called Ridley's with a chrome depiction of Marilyn Monroe from the Airvent Period. I'm fairly certain Peg took it—either to spite me, or to sell." Mungo leaned forward. "I assume Peg has . . . talked to you about this?"

Solemnly Daisy shook her head. " "No, Mungo. Peg only talks to me about her sewing."

"Well, what you have to understand is that this 'cap is the crown jewel of my collection, with an appraised value of over $3,000. Peg needs to be told that if I do not get it back, I intend to prosecute to the fullest extent of the law."

"Mungo, this sounds serious."

Mungo raised his chin. "That is correct. This is very serious. And I hope you will convey to Peg how serious I am."

"Mungo, no!" Daisy balled her hands into little pink fists. "I will not be the go-between for your divorce. And if you two make me choose sides, I'll be so angry, I'll—I'll fire you both. Now *please* don't make me do this."

Mungo was bewildered. "So what do I do with the alpaca?"

"Oh, Mungo. Please!"

He prodded gently. "It's a nice piece, Miss Daisy. It's got places we could make up bias, if I could just clear my head."

"Oh, Mungo." Daisy blinked helplessly and sighed. "Just this once, do you hear?" She looked at her schedule. "Peg didn't come in today, did she?"

"She did not."

"Then I'll talk to her Monday."

"Dandy." Mungo grunted and got up, smoothing the front of his jeans. "Is my good buddy Leo coming by this evening?"

Casually, Daisy picked up her enameled carrot pen. "Probably not, Mungo. Leo's very busy with his new coffee. We're going to sample it tonight.''

"Then could you tell him I'm looking for him?''

"Thank you, Mungo. I will.''

"On the contrary, Miss Daisy, thank *you*.''

2

It was the only cupping table north of San Francisco. Built by Great-Grandpa Oliveri in the thirties when there was still such a thing as blond walnut, it was modeled after a famous round table in Milan.

Nine feet across, the polished boards were a starburst pattern of twelve veneer wedges trimmed with a fat brass rail. Welded into the rail were lacquered spittoon cups—like old-timey hearing funnels—that channeled spat coffee straight to the sewer. Around the table were twelve rolling leather chairs that generations of Oliveri children had used for racing.

Teddy and Aurie Scholl gazed through the plate glass of the roasting room to the magnificent table at the far end. Lab-coated and bow-tied, the balding Mr. Oliveri looked up and smiled. Teddy waved cheerfully through the glass and the coffeeman pointed to a door in the lobby marked *Staff Only.* They walked over and waited.

Aurie pushed his glasses up his beaked Gallic nose and combed his brown hair straight back with his fingers. "How did a guy like Leo get hooked up with the Oliveris? I thought they were your mother's friends."

"Daisy introduced them. AgroGene specified that a coffee specialist be involved in the drying and roasting since it's so labor-intensive. Mr. Oliveri is written into the contract."

9

"The Oliveris have as many kids as your family, right?" asked Aurie.

"Beat us by two."

"*Nine* children?"

Teddy nodded. "Marmee and Mrs. Oliveri say they used to see each other coming and going at the maternity ward. Our Carlo and their Louie were born two days apart."

Aurie inspected her flannel slacks and high-necked sweater. He moved in close, towering over her by at least eight inches. "Want to go back to my place after the cupping? I could show you what they're doing to the hot tub."

Teddy stepped back casually. "Thank you, Aurie. But I don't think so. I have to go back home to Bellingham tonight and finish grading."

"Just checking."

"I know."

They listened as Mr. Oliveri whistled in the hallway, then swung open the door. "Teodora!" Mr. Oliveri flashed his perfect white teeth. "What a treat. You girls get prettier every time I see you."

"Thank you, Mr. Oliveri!"

The coffee man raised his eyebrows wistfully. "My mother was Teodora."

"Is that right?"

"Her brother's Guistino. After the mosaics in Ravenna."

Teddy smiled. "I must see them sometime."

"You must see them sometime."

Teddy touched Aurie on the arm. "Mr. Oliveri, I'd like you to meet my friend Aurie Scholl. He's a knee surgeon, he works with the Seahawks."

"Oh, yes! Your partner did my son last summer—Dr. Molaski."

"Ted." Aurie put out his hand. "Does great work."

"You betcha. Louie was up fencing again in four weeks." Mr. Oliveri waved them in. "And Teodora, how's *your* mother these days?"

"In the Galapagos right now. On tour with Elderhostel."

"That! Irene wants me to do that."

"You should."

"Oh, you betcha." Mr. Oliveri gestured to the spanking new wainscoting on either side of the hall. "The accountant told me not to miss a day of work until I'm seventy-two."

"Not to mention that the only way you'd ever leave here is in a box."

"Or a sack." The coffee man shrugged. "An old sack would be fine." He led them into the warehouse area and they filed through mountains of jute bags stacked on pallets. Stencilled on the jute were coffee words from the entire planet—Santos, Malabar, Préjean et Cie, Antigua, Supremo, Fazenda da Silva, Harrar, Mezzana Estate.

Aurie sniffed. "Doesn't smell like coffee." It smelled of earth and grass.

"Not until you roast it," said Mr. Oliveri. "Teddy, you didn't see your brilliant brother-in-law out in the parking lot, did you?"

"No. No Leo out there."

They entered the glass-enclosed roasting room with its spectacular two-story green enamel roaster. Ignoring the bank-owned beauty, Mr. Oliveri gestured to three stainless pans on his revolving work table. The pans were heaped with fragrant, freshly roasted beans. "I don't know what Leo wants to cup with his experiment beans, so I just put out two mochas."

Teddy and Aurie walked over to inspect the beans. The three samples seemed identical, parched to perfection in the signature Oliveri roast—dark brown, wide-cracked, oily caffeol barely flushed to the surface.

"Which one is Leo's?" Teddy asked.

"On the end. He calls it R-19."

She bent down to sniff. "I smell it!"

"It's good, huh?" said Oliveri.

Aurie sniffed, too. "Wow."

"Now I get it!" She looked up. "Leo wasn't after a Hershey's or a Belgian kind of thing at all. This is more like"— she sniffed again—"*earth* chocolate."

Oliveri laughed. "He used for his material El Beso chocolate, from the Venezuelan north slope."

"Is that"—Teddy didn't know how to cage words in this profession—"the best chocolate in the world, in your opinion?"

"In my opinion it is the chocolate they sold in the Garden of Eden." Oliveri set out six linen napkins, and six water glasses on doilies. Then, on porcelain spoon rests, he nestled antique silver cupping spoons.

Teddy admired the table settings. "The spoons are called something . . ."

"*Goûte-cafés*. I call them spoons."

"May we help?"

"No, no." Oliveri filled a water pitcher. "This part I enjoy."

Aurie pinched one of Leo's beans and sniffed his fingers. "May I ask a question?"

"Of course, Dr. Molaski."

Aurie blinked. "Scholl, Aurie Scholl."

"Dr. Scholl. Yes?"

"Why are we tasting two other coffees if we already know Leo's is more chocolatey?"

Oliveri shook a pan of beans. "There are a million things to taste for—too thin, too bitter, no acid. We drink Leo's with the other two because we know they're nice."

"No *acid*?"

"Not what you think." Mr. Oliveri set out a long row of white handleless cups on his revolving table. "Acid is the sparkle—prickly on the sides of your tongue." With his fingers in a V, he indicated two separate areas on each side of his tongue.

Aurie touched one of other pans. "So this, for instance, what's this?"

"That is . . . a peaberry maragogypre from Fazenda Pereira in Brazil."

"Fa—?"

"Fazenda. It means plantation, or farm. The Pereiras were our Louie's host family last year in Brazil. They send me perfect, always."

"And this, what's this?" Aurie shook the second bowl.

Mr. Oliveri's dark eyes gleamed with pleasure. "Shhh. That one's a secret." He whispered. "That's the Ethiopian mocha that Leo used for genetic base. It's from the Ahmar mountains, in the east."

"Oh." Aurie whispered too. Across the room, the fire exit rattled.

Mr. Oliveri growled. "He's back!"

"I'll get it." Aurie loped over to the metal door.

Teddy murmured, "Who's back?"

"Leo's intern boy." Oliveri turned away peevishly. "He's been here all week, he's driving me crazy."

Aurie held open the door for a yuppie mountaineer who strode purposefully across the waxed concrete. Mr. Oliveri sighed. "Kevin, I'd like you to meet Leo Faber's sister-in-law, Teddy Morelli." Mr. Oliveri turned to Aurie, "And this is her friend, Dr . . ."

"Aurie Scholl."

"Aurie Scholl," repeated Mr. Oliveri. "Friends, this is Kevin Hyatt, he's doing an internship with Leo."

"How do you do?" Kevin was upscale, mid-twenties, and vaguely East Coasty. He had a thick mop of well-cut hair, and his nylon Euro-parka fell fashionably off his shoulders. His khakis were blade-sharp, straight from the cleaners, and his soft leather ankle boots had not yet seen weather.

"I'm fine, thank you," said Teddy.

Aurie said, "What is an internship, anyway? I thought all Leo's slaves were graduate students?"

Kevin brightened. "I work for AgroGene-Boston, it's an agricultural research company."

"And what do you do at AgroGene?"

Kevin snapped to attention. "AgroGene is in the business of creating mutually beneficial partnerships of the mind between research universities—like Dr. Faber's—and the agricultural biotechnology community."

Everyone looked away, embarrassed.

Teddy added kindly, "AgroGene is Leo's funding source, Aurie."

"Oh, I get it," said Aurie. "You're the spy."

Kevin forced a smile.

Aurie continued, to indicate he had nothing against spying. "But what do you get out this? You working on a B.S. or something?"

Stiffly Kevin said, "I did a B.S. in horticulture, then my coffee year in Brazil. Eventually I hope to go on for an M.B.A."

"I like the sound of that: coffee year in Brazil." Aurie sidled up, trying to make friends again. "What is that, some kind of excuse to do Carnival?"

"I wish." Kevin grinned. "I worked my tail off in Brazil."

Teddy glanced at their neglected host. "Louie just did a coffee year, didn't he, Mr. Oliveri?"

"You betcha. Especially the Carnival part. Which reminds me, he said you're judging the dance contest next week at Seattle U. That's a *nice* thing to do on your spring break."

"Ha!" Teddy raised her eyebrows. "Is that what he called it? He just didn't want his father to know how they raise money these days."

"And how's that?"

"Well, this one is put on by the Asian Students Union, it's called the Miss Asia Pageant."

Oliveri nodded. "A beauty contest."

"Sort of. Asian boys dress up in drag and compete in three categories: ballgown, talent, interview. They're using gymnastic scoring, so Louie asked me to judge."

Mr. Oliveri sighed. "And they all think they're so brand-new, don't they?'' He glanced up at the clock.

Aurie slipped his hands in his pockets and chummed again with Kevin. "So tell me, is it possible to explain what Leo's done here tonight—or will I not understand a word you're saying?''

Kevin exhaled. "Leo has basically . . . tasked two separate things.'' He hesitated. "The first part of the work was to clone the thiazole precursor from a preferred South American cocoa strain—I'm sorry, I'm not allowed to tell you which one—and introduce it into the DNA of a very select African *arabica* that already had a high concentration of thiazole to begin with—and again, I'm sorry, I'm not at liberty to tell you which mocha he used for gene material.''

Teddy glanced at Mr. Oliveri, who innocently sniffed the steam over the electric kettle.

"Thiazole is the taste in cocoa?'' asked Aurie.

Kevin opened his mouth, then finally said, "One of them.''

"You said Leo's done two things . . .''

"Yes. When Dr. Faber talked to coffee people''—Kevin glanced at Mr. Oliveri—"they told him a genuine chocolate coffee would have to be very mild, with no trace of bitterness.'' Kevin stuck out his tongue and pointed to the back. "And since caffeine is the chief culprit for bitterness, the second thing Dr. Faber tasked was to infect the caffeine catabolizing gene—he called it CAF—with a commercial lab virus that speeds up the breakdown of caffeine as the coffee matures.''

"Wait a minute.'' Teddy screwed up her face. "You just said coffee *ca*tabolizes caffeine as it matures. You mean it make *less* caffeine as it gets older?''

"That's right.'' Kevin nodded. "Caffeine is at its highest when the plant is young and tender. It's the plant's natural insecticide.''

"Yuck!''

"Shhh.'' Mr. Oliveri leaned forward. "Don't tell the customers.''

Kevin laughed and adjusted the chunky gold watch on his wrist. "Basically caffeine's a poison. That's why it gets your heart going. It's in a class of alkaloids that protects plants from insects. Nicotine's another."

"Don't worry," Mr. Oliveri sniffed his coffee grinder and then the inside of the grinder lid. "Humans are too big for caffeine. You would have to drink a hundred cups in a row for it to kill you."

"Without excreting any," added Kevin.

"Without excreting any."

Suddenly in the lobby flashed a whirlwind of color. Daisy entered in a brilliant coral dress and high heels, a trenchcoat thrown over her shoulders. Her cheeks and lips were barely tinted a complimentary shade and her gleaming brown hair was swept up off her face.

"I'll go get the door." Teddy scurried out through the warehouse and pressed the doorbar to let her sister in. "Daisy, you look great!"

Daisy smelled faintly of Joy, which Leo had given her last Christmas. She hugged her sister. "Do you really think so? Teddy, I decided you were right—I'm just imagining all this about Leo. *My* problem is that I'm too close to forty."

Teddy snapped her neck around like a daytime TV hostess. "Girlfrien', if I look like *that* when I'm forty, I be a happy woman." She lowered her voice, "I can't wait to see Leo's face when he walks in. He won't know what hit him."

Daisy let out a crystal giggle.

They quieted themselves as they strolled through the warehouse, coming into the roasting room as Mr. Oliveri was finishing: ". . . I told Leo: come see me after you pick five pounds of coffee cherries, then I'll roast you up one good pound of beans. Hi, Daisy. You look pretty as Christmas."

"Thank you, Mr. Oliveri! How are you?"

"Just dandy. No Leo with you, huh?"

Daisy smoothed her dress. "He's going to meet me here."

The coffee man looked around, "Daisy, you know every-one—Kevin Hyatt from the lab?"

"Of course. Hi, Kevin."

"Hello, Mrs. Faber." Kevin turned away quickly.

Mr. Oliveri examined the splendidly set table—deep-bowled cupping spoons, linen napkins, an arc of doilied water glasses—and he glanced again at the clock. "Well, Daisy, what do you say? Should we call him at the lab?"

She pushed her gold bracelets up her arm. "Five more minutes."

They all waited—Teddy, Aurie, Daisy, and Kevin, watching Mr. Oliveri rearrange the beans, sniff the roiling two hundred-degree water, wipe invisible dust off the table. He suddenly noticed an imperfection on the flawless enamel roaster and dashed over to polish it with a towel.

"The roaster's new, isn't it?" said Teddy.

"We should have bought a bigger one already."

Aurie asked, "The coffee boom hit you by surprise?"

"Oh, we knew it was coming." Oliveri polished the dealer's plaque. "My father—back in the sixties when Pike Place almost closed down—my father brings in the Coffee Bureau Yearbook—1967, I remember—and shows me: the highest national consumption is Caucasian forty- to forty-nine-year-olds in Western states—and my father says, "Luigi, when today's young people are forty, I want you to be there.' And I said, 'Sure, Pop, I can do that.' "

Mr. Oliveri craned his neck to inspect the magnificent roaster. "So, here we are."

Suddenly the lobby door swung open and Leo walked in escorting an adorable young redhead. She was willowy and slim with a thick copper braid and high rounded breasts; Leo's hand was in the small of her back.

Daisy let out a cry like a dying bird.

Finally Aurie blurted, "I'll get the door." He loped out, leaving Mr. Oliveri, Teddy, Kevin, and Daisy stunned and silent, not daring to look at one another. They listened to the buoyant voices pass through the warehouse, then burst into the roasting room.

"Hello, people." Leo and his companion entered smiling. Up close she had a sprinkle of russet freckles and jade green eyes. She wore ivory jeans and Birkenstocks, and under her celadon sweater her melony breasts were offered up by a clever bra.

"People"—Leo held up his hands. "I'd like you to meet my new lab assistant, Molly Thistle." He gazed as if she had fallen off the ceiling of the Sistine Chapel. "Molly had a lot to do with getting us here tonight, and I thought she should be allowed to savor the reward."

Pretty Molly Thistle shook hands with *almost* everyone while Leo walked over to peck Daisy on the cheek. "Hello, dear. How was your day?" He didn't wait for an answer, only paced to the head of the table and rolled back the chair next to Mr. Oliveri's. "Molly?"

The group watched as Leo helped her sit, then sat beside her.

Like sleepwalkers, everyone else shuffled to the table— everyone except Daisy, who didn't move. Instantly Aurie scooped her under his arm and seated her as far away from Leo as possible. Loping over to the sideboard, he collected another place setting for himself—water glass, napkin, spoon rest, cupping spoon—and set up next to Daisy. Swiftly Teddy settled in on Daisy's other side.

Uncertain where to sit, Kevin Hyatt finally positioned himself next to Leo, effectively dividing the table into two hostile camps: Daisy, Teddy, and Aurie on the Oliveri right; Molly, Leo, Kevin on his left. The silence was gray pudding.

Supremely aware, Molly Thistle picked up her silver cupping spoon and examined the scalloped bowl. Then she turned it over to inspect the foreign hallmarks.

Panicky, Mr. Oliveri looked at Leo. "Everything's all right?" He strode to the counter.

"Maestro, fine! Let's get started." Leo rolled his chair

around to watch the first bowl of beans slide into the grinder. He was wearing one of his new custom-made shirts from Albert, Ltd.—a deceptively simple blue oxford cloth—and his tiny ovoid glasses made him look brainy and stylish. "What are we cupping the R-19 with tonight?"

Mr. Oliveri nodded to the grinder, "Brazilian, and an Ethiopian."

"The Ahmar?"

"Yes."

"Perfect." He glanced at Molly Thistle to make sure she was happy; Molly, in turn, examined the two sisters, not quite certain which one was the wife. She smiled benignly, to help them adapt to this new situation, the natural order of things.

There was a long silence, and finally Aurie leaned his elbows on the table. "Leo, old man, how much would you say this scandal costs per pound?"

Leo shuddered. "Horrible question. Makes me want to crawl under the table. Kevin, how about you? You're keeping tabs better than I."

"I try not to think about it."

Next Aurie turned sweetly to Molly Thistle, "And how long have you been working for this reprobate?"

"Three months."

"Are you back in his cloning lab or over at tissue culture?"

The poised, adorable redhead framed her answer. "I only work part-time, so I end up doing a little bit of everything. My 'day job' "—she gave it air quotes—"is in art and marketing at the Body Royal Nutrition Center. We serve the bulimic-anorexic community."

Aurie perked up. "You've found ways to make them eat?"

Molly frowned. "You see? There's still immense discrimination against B.A.'s as a special-needs community. What we do at Body Royal is develop alternative nutritional delivery systems."

"Al . . . ternative?"

Molly nodded. "Colonics, transdermals, subcutaneous. Very"—air quotes again—"'cutting edge.' Our best-seller so far has been our shiitake mushroom suppositories. We're currently working on a shiitake skin patch."

"A shiitake skin patch . . ." Aurie pushed his glasses up his nose. "I feel so inadequate . . ."

"Yes." Molly raised her chin. "Mushroom research is really quite exciting. Shiitakes contain wonderful antitumor stuff for T-cells and things."

"Say, you weren't the folks with the ginseng suppositories last year, were you?"

Molly colored. "Her bleeding was *strictly* from overuse."

"But you've taken them off the market?"

The pretty redhead glanced forlornly at Leo, who patted her hand consolingly. "It's okay, dear." He narrowed his eyes at Aurie. "*I'm* consulting with Body Royal now. There'll be no more colonic ginseng."

Molly smiled gratefully.

Across the room Mr. Oliveri weighed out fresh Brazilian grinds into the handleless white cups—tapping the scale to get exactly seven and one-half ounces each time. Then, revolving his circular work table with one hand, he poured hot water into the cups and set them on a Moroccan teacart. He repeated the grinding and the measuring with the Ethiopian coffee, and then Leo's R-19.

Pushing the cart across the room, he set out the three frothy brews in front of each guest. "Wait a bit, it needs to set up." In front of his own chair, he put out six cups, two of each sample.

"Maestro, there's a reason you're getting two of each."

"Samples vary, Leo. I give you two if you want them."

"No, no. This is fine." Leo picked up his cupping spoon, uncertain what to do.

"How do we keep them straight?" asked Molly Thistle.

Oliveri pointed. "Brazilian, Ethiopian, R-19. If you get mixed up, ask, I'll tell you what you're drinking."

In an eyeblink Mr. Oliveri had rolled his chair to the table, tucked his glasses in his pocket, and hunched over his coffees with his cupping spoon. "Don't drink yet, it's too hot." Swiftly he ladled coffees to his nose, over and over, sniffing and scooping in a quick repetitive motion. He was working now, unaware that anyone else was in the room.

"Well, what do you think?" asked Leo.

Oliveri shrugged. "Sweet. Chocolate." He scooped up Ethiopian, Brazilian, R-19 again. "Do you like your grinds, Leo?"

"I don't know. Do I?"

"Yes. Like river silt."

Teddy picked up her spoon and broke through the black oily grinds on top of R-19. She sniffed the brew and it smelled like the inside of a chocolate box. But then came the vanilla, and her mind flashed on the image of a yellow jewel . . . citrine. Citrine? She ladled again and sniffed. This time it was blue. She put down her spoon, confused.

Mr. Oliveri rolled back his chair to turn off the gas burner under the water. "Give it time to cool a bit, you'll burn your tongue." He pulled a clipboard from the shelf, then rolled up to the cupping table again, all business. Touching the R-19 onto his lip, he blew, then slurped coffee with an appalling noise. They waited.

Rolling coffee around his mouth, Mr. Oliveri broke into a wry smile. He spat. "Leo."

"You like it."

Oliveri shrugged. "It does the job."

Leo raised his arms and looked at the ceiling. "Thank you, Jesus!"

Molly grabbed Mr. Oliveri's arm. "What does it taste like?"

"Nice. The acid's lovely, very bright." The coffee man dipped his spoon into the Ethiopian, cooled it and once again did his horrendous slurp. He spat. "Yes, acid's comparable, a little mild. Leo, how'd you get that good acid in a green-house?''

With a glazed smile Leo picked up his own spoon and dipped into R-19. Blowing on it gently, he said, "I can't believe you like it.''

"I like it.''

Everyone else dipped his spoon, cooled the coffee, and tasted. Teddy slurped like Mr. Oliveri and ended up choking.

"Good fragrance," said Aurie. "Floral." He was way out of his element.

Kevin Hyatt used his spittoon. "You mean aroma, Dr. Scholl. Fragrance is a word for the beans.''

"What's nose, then?" Aurie turned to show his beaked Gallic profile. "I do great nose.''

They laughed and Teddy slurped her Brazilian, her Ethiopian, her R-19, always swallowing, forgetting the spittoon. All three coffees were prickly and bright, reminding her of rainy Seattle mornings and Marmee's kitchen. But R-19 was something else—chocolate, childhood, a secret garden of half-forgotten pleasures. She cleansed her mouth between slurps, and the water tasted as bright as a soft drink on the sides of her tongue.

Beside her Mr. Oliveri pulled his clipboard close. Teddy read: "Coffee Flavor Profile." On the sheet was a rectangular grid labeled across the top from 1 to 5 and down the sides: "fragrance, aroma, nose, taints, body, aftertaste, mouthfeel, faults, acidity." Oliveri picked up his pencil. "Leo, you want me to chart, is that right?''

Leo bowed his head respectfully. "Maestro, if you please.''

"No problem." Mr. Oliveri drew a quick jagged line down the cupping form rating R-19 with a spicy fragrance, a fruity aroma, a caramelly-nutty nose—each trait ranked at "4." Then his line zipped back to "0" for taints, a "4" for body and aftertaste, and then out to "5"—underlined—for its good chocolate taste and acidity. Leo watched with the stunned pleasure of a man who had won the lottery. "Could you sign it, please?"

"No problem." Mr. Oliveri scribbled at the bottom and murmured. "I still want to know how you got the acid in a plain old Seattle greenhouse."

Leo shrugged. "Sorry. Security."

Teddy asked, "Why is the good acid so surprising, Mr. Oliveri?"

"Well . . ." The coffee man glanced sideways at Leo. "It's just that I told him, greenhouse coffee is wood pulp. He's never going to get good taste in his university greenhouse." He gazed directly at Leo. "Tell me, I keep a secret."

Leo rested his weary head against the oiled leather and cleared his throat, speaking for posterity. "Let's just say that we old-fashioned bench botanists have finally learned to provide stressors *in vitro*, just as in real life. Heat, cold, less than optimal feedings—those are things that build character." He glanced across at his wife, "Isn't that right, dear?"

Everyone looked at Daisy. Her coffees sat untouched on the table.

"Well! Fine!" Mr. Oliveri slapped his knee, rolling back his chair. "When do you two make your grand announcement?"

Leo glanced at Kevin. "No time soon, I should think. We still have plenty of work to do, don't we, Kevin?"

"I'll say."

Leo settled in, tenting his fingertips together. "First thing I have to do is pow-wow with my dean, start talking patents and percentages. Then"—he sighed—"we start farming it out big-time, make sure we can get some product consistency." His eyes looked off into vast unseen greenhouses of R-19, and he glanced wearily at Kevin. "I guess AgroGene will want to write themselves a bigger role now."

Kevin raised his eyebrows. "They've already asked me when they can send out marketing people." He pointed to the cupping form on Mr. Oliveri's clipboard. "May I make a copy of that? I need to fax it out for Monday."

Mr. Oliveri pulled it off his clipboard. "No problem."

"So . . ." Teddy shifted in her chair. "The world's first natural mocha. There's really a big market for that, isn't there?"

Leo and Kevin burst out in nervous laughter. "We can always hope, can't we, Kevin?"

Kevin cleared his throat and tucked his hands neatly under his thighs. "I think you're being too modest, Dr. Faber."

Leo dabbed his mouth and dropped the linen square on the table. "Words fail me."

From the corner of his eye, Kevin looked admiringly at Leo, then glanced at Teddy. "I know he won't say anything because we're still in research phase, but what Dr. Faber's not telling you right now is that he's possibly just invented the first ten-billion-dollar coffee."

3

Teddy sat up. "You don't really mean that? *Ten* billion dollars?"

"Per year. Do the math." Kevin picked up his pencil. "Brazil ships thirty million sacks a year. Hundred and thirty-two pounds per sack. Wholesale that about five dollars a pound. I come up with an awful lot of zeros."

Leo cleared his throat. "Kevin's being too kind. And perhaps a little too precipitous. I hope you'll all understand that no one says a *word* until I've talked to my dean. Daisy, I wish you would have invited him like I asked."

Daisy stood, her voice a deaf-mute monotone. "Leo, when are you coming home?"

It was horrible to endure.

Reaching to scratch his nose, Leo covered his face. "Not 'til late, dear. I have to go back to the lab."

Molly Thistle agreed with bright innocent eyes.

Aurie, too, stood. "Daisy, I'm dropping Teddy off at your house anyway, why don't we take you home?"

Daisy's eyes were lusterless brown, the pupils bare pinpoints of life. "But I have the Mercedes."

"Teddy can drive it. She'll follow."

"You bet." Teddy dipped into her sister's purse for the

blue leather key case. "I'd love to drive something big and decadent for a change."

They shuttled Daisy out, making quick goodbyes.

Aurie squired Daisy into the passenger seat of his brown Saab, then reached over to buckle her in. Teddy followed them north across the Aurora bridge, and over the interstate to the landscaped neighborhoods overlooking Lake Washington.

Aurie pulled into the near vertical driveway at Daisy's house, and set the parking brake, hard. Teddy took a long time parking down on the street—well beyond her own car—and angled the tires of Daisy's yellow Mercedes into the curb. Then she trudged up the twenty-seven rock steps cut into the cliff that was Daisy's front yard.

The door was still unlocked so Teddy went in, walking to the back of the house where she knew they'd be. Passing through the living room, she smiled—as did everyone in Daisy's house—at former best-selling bunnies plopped around like sofa pillows: Peterkins, Proud Mary, Scarlett O'Hare-a. Next to the piano stood five-foot-tall Arthur Rabbitstein, urbane and competent in his black tie and tails.

Back in the sunroom Daisy stood looking across Lake Washington at the lights on the other side. The lake was a gray hole, same color as the sky, and with very little imagination the lighted suburbs became suspended in space—like a *Star Wars* city. Aurie stood helplessly in the corner, his arms folded.

Teddy examined her sister's face. "Daisy," she said. "Do you want me to help you get ready for bed?"

"No, thank you."

"Can we do anything for you?"

"How about throwing me off the cliff?" Daisy plunked down in the rocker, smashing Bunnikins into the slats. She brought her knees up to her chin and stared out at the lake. "Ignore me. I'm fine."

"No, you're not."

Daisy rocked defiantly. "I'd just like to sit here a while, if you don't mind. You two can go."

"You sure we can't do anything?"

She bludgeoned them with a smile. "No, thank you. Thank you, Aurie, for bringing me home."

"My pleasure."

The air was suffocating, Teddy eased open the casement. "Your car's on the street. I left your keys on the hall table."

"Thank you. Are you still driving back to Bellingham tonight, Teddy?"

"Yes, I'm sorry. I need to grade exams for Monday."

"Nothing to be sorry about." Daisy blinked sweetly. "Well, good night, Aurie."

Teddy choked, then started again. "I'll be back in a bit, okay? I'm going to walk Aurie out." She forced a smile. "Don't worry, did you see she had Birkenstocks?"

Daisy shut her eyes. "Good night."

They walked outside, and gulped air.

"God!" Aurie combed back his hair from his forehead. "What a tool! How could he just sit there and do that?"

Teddy wrapped her arms around his torso. "Aurie, thank you so much. That was genuinely kind, with Daisy."

Aurie stuffed his hands into the pockets of his leather bomber jacket and looked around. "Come on, I need a walk. Where can we go?"

Teddy surveyed the sleek sixties houses and gardener-stunted trees. At the end of the manicured cul-de-sac was the only stretch of unkempt landscape, the public right-of-way. "We could walk down to Matthews Beach in about twenty minutes. But we'll have to walk up again."

"Won't kill us."

They headed toward the hidden neighborhood stairs and bounded down. Coming out on a lower street, they trounced the concrete hill, working their way down more stairs, more steep streets, and still more rights-of-way. Crossing the boulevard, they jogged to the hidden pocket park on the edge of

Lake Washington. They crossed the playfield and—like everyone who walks to water—made a beeline for the shore.

Up close, the lake was restless and ripply, the surface brushed with city light. High above, dim urban stars pumped what candlepower they could. Orion was there, and the twins from Gemini.

Aurie pointed to Orion. "See the big star below Orion's belt?"

"Betelgeuse."

"Other side."

". . . okay."

"It's called Rigel," he said. "R-I-G-E-L. I just set the tibia of a twelve-year-old Rigel who said she was named after it. She says whenever she needs her own star, she can always look up and find it."

"Nice mom."

Aurie surveyed the flood-gullied field, looking for the best way to walk. "What was the deal about the Birkenstocks? Is that some sort of sisterly code?"

"Forget it. It was a yahoo thing to say." Teddy, too, squinted down in the dim light. Duck scat and downy feathers covered every square foot of lakefront.

"Forgive my ignorance of clothing semiotics, but advertising tells me that Birkenstocks are sturdy and dependable . . ."

Teddy hopped a rain gully and began to walk. "What I meant was that Molly might be a little too counter-culture for Leo. He's very much into his upscale consumption." Deftly she leaped to a large rock.

"Really? I hadn't noticed."

"No, you wouldn't." She twisted around, squinting. "Aurie, our shoes are going to be covered with duck poop."

"Just yours." He pressed the center of her back. "What I want to know is, does this conflict of clothing styles mean that Molly will drop Leo because he's an old fart, or that Leo will drop Molly because her youth exhausts him?"

"I don't know, Aurie. I'm just making this up." She

reached a sandy spot and stopped. "For all I know Leo might have already gone out and bought himself Birkenstocks."

Aurie stepped into the same sandy spot, then set off for a large boulder at water's edge. "Are our shoes compatible?"

Teddy looked down at her man-styled wing-tips rimmed with duck poop, then tried to remember what Aurie had on. "Aurie, think about it: you're wearing French walking shoes named after the devil in *Dr. Faustus*."

He sat down on the boulder and grabbed her hand, making a place for her between his legs. "I like your shoes. They look like baby shoes to me."

She pulled away. "Just another smallish thing to be overcome . . ."

He dropped his hands in his lap. "And that's the other thing. I would like to know why our little *affaire de coeur*, our *ménage á deux*, isn't coming along in . . . a more forwardly progression."

"Let me think." Sarcastically she raised a finger to her cheek. "Could it be because . . . here it is the end of March and I've only seen you four times since Christmas?"

"And when we do get together," he said, "it doesn't feel like we're going anywhere. Now why is that?"

"It's a failing on my part, Aurie."

"But you're going to tell me what I'm doing wrong, aren't you?"

"Nothing, Aurie. You're doing a great job of being Aurie Scholl."

"But you're going to tell me what I'm doing wrong."

Teddy exhaled, fixing her gaze on the starry symmetry of Orion's belt. "Okay, I guess what I'm waiting for is for you to get tired of driving ninety miles to Bellingham 'every other weekend provided I don't have to go to Philadelphia.' "

"There are no more conferences until the fall."

"Aurie, it's an impossible situation. You know that as well as I do."

"You could quit the history department in Bellingham and apply down here."

"That's not funny anymore, Aurie. It makes me want to bite you."

Aurie stood, shoving his hands forlornly into his bomber jacket. "All I know is I *need* your company."

She turned to face him. "Wrong, what you need from women is verbal sparring. It works like foreplay for you." She bit her lip and started walking. "I bet you didn't know that about yourself, did you?"

"Of course I know that!" He paced beside her. "That's a problem? I just think you ought to meet me halfway on this one."

"Aurie, I already sat down with a calendar and realized it would take you about three weekends to get tired of driving an hour and a half for your creature comforts. I mean, so, what's the point? Why not call if off before the three times, rather than after?"

"Three! Three?"

Geese darted from the sawyer grass. Aurie lowered his voice. "Teddy, that's profoundly insulting! I can think of at least a dozen perfectly *unspeakable* things I'd like to do to your little body. He scrunched his face. "I put a lot of thought into these things."

"Aurie, we can't get married."

"Three," he murmured. "Gee, that's scary. And now I can't even ask you home to talk about it because you'll think it's foreplay."

"Also I have to go back tonight."

"Just look how auspicious the constellations are."

"Aurie," she hollered. "One last time: this won't work. We have the long-term prospects of fruit flies."

"I'll still respect you in the morning."

"*Arrgh.*" She stalked across the grass. "I hate this. I always feel like I'm trying to unstick myself from your *mess.*

You're like an octopus, Aurie. You devour everything that comes in your path.''

"My lair. Can we say I devour everything that comes to my lair?''

"Aurie!'' she seethed. "Why can't you take things seriously?''

He smiled, with utmost tenderness. "Adorable little person, if you only knew how serious I am.'' He glanced at his watch. "Look, it's only ten. Why not fly with me to my elfin grot and we'll make cocoa? We can sit on the dock and try to figure out why little Rigel broke her tibia on the exact spot where her star is in Orion.''

"Aurie, I want to go home. I have to back to Bellingham and finish grading.''

"Rats! I blew it. And so close, too.'' He held out a hand to help her cross a gully. "Come on, we better get you back to Daisy's. Is your stuff packed?''

"No. It's all over the front bedroom. I hope she's asleep.''

He craned his neck to look at the lighted hillside above. "We've got quite a climb.''

"Funniest thing about gravity.''

They darted across the boulevard and slipped into the woods, puffing and huffing their way back up to Daisy's. At each manicured intersection, Teddy stopped to divine the correct course. Between streets they climbed stairs and trudged up steep ravines. After thirty minutes they looked down at the lake and saw they were only halfway up.

"Remind me to drive down next time,'' panted Aurie.

"Aurie, I think I'm lost.''

"You're not allowed to be lost.''

They took left turns and right turns, finally stumbling onto a street with pollarded trees. Teddy looked up to see Daisy's sunroom perched on the cliff. "There it is! We've got to go all the way around.''

They turned onto Daisy's block and hiked the last hundred yards, too tired to talk. Tramping past the cars on the street,

Teddy saw that Daisy's Mercedes was slightly lower on the hill and that the tires had been twisted wrong way off the curb. She laughed.

Aurie huffed, "What's so funny?"

"Daisy came down and reparked the car. She didn't trust me."

"She got it backwards."

"I know."

They rounded the corner of the sandstone cliff and suddenly the porch light flashed on. The door banged open, and Daisy dashed out, still in coral shirtwaist and heels. Clopping down the porch steps, she disappeared into the rockery.

"Daisy?" Teddy called.

There was no answer.

Teddy and Aurie walked back to the dark cleft where the rockery steps met the sidewalk. They waited. Daisy's heels echoed off the sandstone walls. Seconds later she dashed out and ran right into Aurie.

"Oh!"

Instantly she recovered and clopped around to the driver's side of the Mercedes. "Teddy, Aurie, hurry. Leo's been hurt at the lab!"

4

"Did you call the EMTs?" asked Aurie.

"No, he called *me*. He said, 'Da-a-zee.' It was awful."

Aurie sprinted up the driveway and pulled his phone from under the front seat. "Daisy, what's campus security?"

"I don't know. Please hurry."

Aurie punched numbers and spoke quietly into the receiver mentioning Leo's greenhouse just off the bike trail, and the possible need for an ambulance. Teddy watched Daisy fidget in the breach of the car door. "He's right, Daisy. If Leo's hurt, he won't be able to let us in."

"Hurry, Aurie," called Daisy.

Aurie pocketed the phone and bolted down the drive, braking his forward progress against Daisy's car hood. "I'm driving." He opened the back door for Daisy.

They made the short trip in silence, pulling up to the greenhouse just as an electric security cart whirred up. On the other side of the ancient holly hedge traffic roared like the Pacific.

The security guard climbed out, jingling his brass bouquet of keys. "You phone?"

"Yes," said Aurie. "You called for an ambulance?"

"On the way."

Daisy dashed to the door of the little brick office anchoring the greenhouse. "It's locked!" She clopped around back, into the specimen camellias and yelled at the window. "Leo?"

No answer. She scurried back to watch the security guard try one key, then another, until he found one that turned in the lock.

Pushing first through the door, Daisy clopped past the long black counters, around the corner to Leo's glassed-in office. She screamed like a woman on fire.

Teddy reached the corner half a second later. Bloody handprints had raked the office glass. Daisy was sunk to her knees. Teddy dashed in and clutched the doorframe as nausea washed from her diaphragm.

On the floor lay Leo, the back of his blue oxford shirt embellished with blooming stab wounds. Some were tiny budlets, where steel hit ribs. Others were the full-throated blooms of June. Under Leo's left scapula there was a strange protrusion, a chrome loop. Teddy gagged, heaving old coffee up her throat. The loop was the single handle of a scissors; the rest of the instrument—including the other handle—was lodged inside Leo's torso.

"Move!" barked Aurie. He dropped to his knees and slipped two long fingers down Leo's neck. He tried another spot, then another. Scanning the body for a hopeful sign, he kept his eyes from Daisy. Finally he stood and mumbled, "Better not touch anything."

Around the corner came the security guard leading an ambulance crew with a gurney. Painfully Daisy stood and cried, "He's dead! She killed him." Teddy could only stare at a small bushy coffee plant spilled on the floor.

The security guard herded them from the doorway, then decided they needed to be entirely outside the building. A city police car pulled up, as did a campus security unit. Teddy moved Daisy to the edge of the sidewalk where they leaned against the bike rack. Emergency personnel swarmed over Aurie, drawn like flies to sugar by his professional vocabulary. Finally a policeman escorted him back inside.

Daisy stared ahead, saying nothing. Teddy kept an arm around her, patting her and keeping her warm. "We'll get you through this, *cara*. We'll get you through this." It was the biggest lie she'd ever told.

A few moments later Aurie came to the door. "Teddy, may I talk to you a minute?"

"I'll be right back, *cara*." She stepped inside where Aurie and several policemen were waiting. Somberly Aurie said, "What do you know about Molly Thistle?"

Teddy shook her head.

"Phone number? Address?"

She shook again.

A policeman stepped forward apologetically. "We'll also be needing a statement from you and Mrs. Faber. I'll turn on the heat in my car, if you want to sit there. We'll be ready in a minute."

"I'll go tell her." Teddy went outside.

Daisy was gone.

"Daisy!" She ran out onto the bike trail. "Daisy?" The pavement was dark and empty in both directions. Suddenly from behind the giant hollies, brakes screeched and horns brayed. Teddy lunged into the thorny hedge, finally pushing through.

Daisy lay on her back in the first lane of traffic, a car honking over her like an angry beast. In other lanes cars began to slow.

"Daisy!"

Teddy made eye contact with the bewildered driver, then pulled Daisy up by the hand. "Daisy, you can't stay here. Get up."

Slowly Daisy sat, puzzled by this nether world. "Fine, thank you. Yes, please. I just need a little rest right now." And she lay back down again.

Aurie placed the brown plastic pill vial in the center of Daisy's kitchen table. Teddy picked it up and read, " 'One tablet at bedtime. Ambien, ten mil.' What's Ambien?''

"For sleep. It's new." Aurie poured his cold coffee into the sink while Teddy watched his reflection in the nighttime glass as he spoke. "They said she'll be out for about ten hours the first time. But her doc wants to know who's going to monitor her medications." He glanced at Teddy.

Teddy checked her watch—3:58 A.M. "Maybe I can get Mrs. Oliveri and the women from church to come over after Mass tomorrow. I've *got* to go home and finish grading."

"Carlo couldn't find your mother?"

"Aurie, it's a sailboat! In the Galapagos!"

"Teddy, it's okay. You're doing everything you can."

She heaved and looked away. "I'll come back as soon as I can—Monday night." Flustered, she picked up the second pill vial and read, " 'Xanax.' That's a tranquilizer, isn't it?"

"Yes."

"And we give her that during the day."

"Correct."

Teddy set the Xanax next to the Ambien, while out in the living room the tambour clock struck four silvery notes. Aurie raked his hair with his fingers and looked across the lake at the constellation of suburban Kirkland. "I've got rounds in the morning." He pulled his bomber jacket off the back of the chair and walked to the front hall. Teddy followed.

He slipped into his coat. "Give her something bland when she gets up. Oatmeal. Rice."

"Fine."

"Call me when you get back in town?" he said.

"Sure."

"I'll come by and check on you guys." Wearily he leaned over and kissed her. "You take care of yourself, you hear? Low and slow."

She nodded. "I know. Thank you, Aurie. Thanks for everything.

"Hmm." Wearily he shuffled down the drive and disappeared around the bluff. As the Saab whined down the hill,

Teddy locked the deadbolt, switched off the light, and turned to climb the stairs. Suddenly yellow air blitzed the front hall as headlights swung into the drive. A dark sedan jerked to a halt and four men sprang from the car. The two in front were policemen.

The men rushed the porch and Teddy scanned their faces. Besides the policemen there were Kevin Hyatt, his hair mussed from sleep, and a handsome middle-aged gent in a Gore-tex fishing jacket. The gent looked through the etched glass apologetically, then rang the bell.

She opened the door. "Yes?"

Gore-tex was in charge. "Mrs. Faber? My name is Michael Havenaw, dean for Academic Research . . ."

"Mrs.—" Kevin interrupted. "She's—"

Teddy answered for both of them. "*Mrs*. Faber is upstairs asleep. I'm her sister."

"May we come in?" Panic reigned in Michael Havenaw's eyes.

She looked at the cops. They weren't real cops, they were campus security. "Certainly." She led them back to the kitchen where the cops stood by the windows gawking at the view.

"Please sit down." She gestured to Daisy's white-stained French Provincial table.

The two cops responded by crossing their arms. Havenaw and Kevin pulled out chairs and sat on the edges.

"I'm sorry, I didn't get your name," said Havenaw.

"Teddy Morelli."

"Teddy," Havenaw beamed professionally. "And you know Dr. Faber's intern, Kevin Hyatt?"

"Yes." Both smiled stiffly.

"Have the police been here?"

Teddy shook her head. "They're coming tomorrow."

Dean Havenaw looked at the pill vials. "Mrs. Faber's sedated?"

"Yes. She won't be up until"—Teddy glanced at the

clock—"one tomorrow afternoon." She waited.

Havenaw and Kevin waited. The campus cops stared into deep space, indicating they were not really in the room. Finally Havenaw blurted, "We don't care whatever else Dr. Faber's got down there, but we do need the R-19."

Teddy leaped up. "It's here? Why isn't it at the lab? I saw *one* plant on the fl—"

"That's not it," said Havenaw.

Kevin popped up and strode over to the basement door. "Dr. Faber always keeps the"—he hesitated—"experimental plants in the basement. He was worried about theft at school."

"Yes," assured Havenaw. "We're not interested in *anything* else that's there," He, too, hovered at the door.

One of the cop reassured, "We're just security officers, ma'am, we don't have the right to observe illegal activity off campus."

"What?"

No one answered, they glared at the basement door.

Teddy swept past the men and opened the door, flipping on the stairway light. Cool basement air rushed up, smelling of Tide and bleach and musty concrete. Leading the men noisily down, she turned and asked, "How could someone steal R-19? It's useless without its patents, isn't it?"

A cop answered. "Not that so much, ma'am, they also steal growlights."

Kevin added, "It's so bad on campus that Dr. Faber says he picks up most of his best lights at police auctions. Like a recycling program."

"Then it's smart of Leo to have kept his good stuff here." Teddy led them across the laundry room to Leo's workshop door. She twisted the knob but was stopped by a deadbolt at eye level. "It's locked."

"Of course it's locked."

"Keys'd be on the body," murmured a cop.

"Wife?"

"Daisy's keys are upstairs, just a minute." Teddy dashed up to the front hall and then remembered that Daisy's blue leather key case was in her own coat pocket, from driving back from campus. She fished it out of the closet and pounced back down to the basement. "Found it."

Opening the case, she sorted through keys. She ignored the two sets of car keys and began poking others in the lock. None worked.

"May I?" asked a cop.

She handed him the case—a soft leather, Matisse blue. Without even trying a single key, the cop picked through and said, "It's not here."

"Damn."

"These units come with two keys. If the professor's got one on his person, the other has to be someplace."

"His desk at work?"

All the men turned to Kevin.

"No. I told you: once he had to call here and ask Mrs. Faber to turn on the fans in the basement. There's got to be a key here."

They all turned to Teddy. "I don't know. Let me think." She looked around the room to think where Leo would have hidden a key—but no, the key at home would have been Daisy's. Picturing Daisy in this room, she walked immediately over to the detergent shelf above the washing machine. There was Tide, borax, bleach, Mrs. Hulling's Bluing, and a pencil can with scissors and a tired toothbrush. Stretching for the pencil can, she peeked in and found a fat brass key. She rattled the can for them.

"Excellent!"

She gave the key to one of the cops and he turned the deadbolt, swinging open the door. The men rushed in and batted the light switch.

Long vinyl-clad tables filled the room, green-shaded grow-lights hung from the ceiling. The tables were empty.

Kevin ran across the floor and threw open the door on the other side. Garage air gushed in.

"Where's the coffee?" blurted Havenaw. He turned to Kevin. "Where's the coffee?"

Kevin spun around. "Somewhere. He took it somewhere. He never kept it in the lab after plantlet stage."

Teddy glanced around the room. The black sheet vinyl covering the tables had been coaxed into perfect upholstery corners and stapled smoothly underneath. Daisy's work.

The four men took turns peering under the tables, into the garage, through the high basement window into the night. Havenaw squinted at the black glass. "Is there a greenhouse out back?"

Teddy jerked her eyes from the pleated black corners. "No, there's ten feet of grass, then a cliff."

The men walked in circles for a few minutes, then tramped abruptly up the stairs, huffing goodbyes. Teddy locked the door behind them and dropped the keycase on the hall table. The tambour clock chimed five.

Much too soon the alarm woke Teddy from a bottomless sleep. She sat up—morning, but she had not set the alarm. It was the doorbell downstairs.

Dashing across to Daisy's room, she pulled a sweatshirt from the drawer and tugged it over her pajamas. The drugged cloud of air over Daisy smelled like synthetic tarps from camping. Teddy scurried downstairs and spied Mungo Henley on the porch. He straightened his back as she opened the door.

"Morning, Miss Teddy. Is Leo here?"

Teddy stared, dumbfounded. "Leo's dead, Mungo." Unbelievable words, like an anvil from space.

"Oh, Jeez!" Unseeing, Mungo staggered into the hall. "Oh, Jeez. And now she's left town, too." He slumped into the black Hitchcock chair.

"No, she's not. She's upstairs asleep."

"Not her—Peg! Peg's gone, and she's taken my hubcap with her!"

Teddy grabbed the stairpost so she would not hit him. "Mungo, you'll have to go. I can't deal with you right now."

"Well, you better learn, quick." Mungo stood. "We need to wake up Miss Daisy."

"Don't you dare! She's sedated. She won't be up for five hours."

"Oh, Jeez," he said. "Then we'll have to wait, won't we? I guess we got a little time." He walked back to the kitchen and looked around, letting his eyes adjust to the downy light off the white-washed cabinets and the lake.

"You hungry?" he said. "I'll make us some coffee. Maybe we can think of something before she gets up."

Teddy collapsed on a chair, watching as he held the water kettle under the tap. "Mungo?"

He put the kettle on the stove. "Now, don't say a word, Miss Teddy, I think I might have blown it."

She blinked, trying to focus her attention on this little man. "Mungo, what are you doing here?"

"Just a minute. I have to think."

She got up and aggressively stood beside him, using the silence to snatch the dirty French press coffee pot and scrape out old grounds. They clung like barnacles. "Mungo," she said, "What does your hubcap have to do with Leo?"

"Did I say that?" Mungo touched his breast pocket for cigarettes that were not there. He grabbed the counter edge and sniffed. "Leo's keys are on the body, I guess?"

"I believe I heard that, yes." Teddy glided over to the freezer and shook out a handful of coffee beans into Daisy's burr grinder. Pressing the starter on the annoying little machine she watched Mungo from the corner of her eye. Something awful was gathering at the edge of her vision.

When the machine was quiet, Mungo snorted. "Well, I guess what we got to do is what we got to do." He pulled out a slip of paper from his wallet and dropped it on the table.

"First of all, I don't exactly know where Peg's gone. And second: even if I did, if *I* went to see her, all I'd get is a black eye. So you—or somebody—is going to have to do this for me."

Teddy shook fresh grinds into the pot. "Pretty soon you're going to tell me what this is all about."

From the front hall a small voice called, "Teddy, who's there?"

Teddy ran to the stairs. "Daisy, you're not supposed to be up."

"I heard voices. Who's back there with you?" Daisy padded down, making her way toward the pearly light. She was wearing a pale yellow bathrobe of quilted satin. Inside, the lining was shocking pink. Mungo instantly evaluated the garment as he grabbed the counter behind him. "Morning, Miss Daisy. If it's any consolation, I hope that little gal of his fries."

Without a word Daisy walked to the window and stared at the snow-capped foothills across the lake. But Mount Rainier was veiled in cloud.

Mungo plucked the slip of paper from the table and held it up like hope. "Miss Daisy, I don't have a phone at my new digs. I was wondering if I could use yours to call up Peg and find out where she is. She has the only other you-know-what to the you-know-where."

Daisy looked right through Mungo. "I already know where she is. She phoned me at dinner yesterday and said she quit."

Mungo snorted. "See what I told ya?" He turned to Teddy. "D'you mind calling? I don't think she'd speak to me."

Teddy raged. "Mungo, I'm not going to do anything until you tell me what's going on. I feel like I'm on the bott—"

"Teddy," said Daisy. "He knows what he's doing."

Mungo grunted and handed Teddy the paper. "It's long distance; 360 is way up there."

"I know. I'm 360 in Bellingham." She punched eleven digits and waited.

"Welcome to Roche Harbor Resort—your call is important to us. Currently, hotel and harbor facilities are operating on a winter schedule. Winter business hours are between nine A.M. and five P.M. Monday through Friday. If you wish to leave a message, you may do so after the beep."

Teddy hung up. "It's the recording for Roche Harbor Resort."

"The what?"

"It's a boat harbor on the north tip of San Juan Island."

"Well, damn it!" Mungo pounded the countertop. "What's she doing up there? Excuse me, I didn't mean to curse."

Daisy stared dreamily out the window. "She and Muriel are opening a teddy bear shop on the island. They want to be ready by summer."

"That is the most confounding woman!" Mungo grabbed his empty shirt pocket.

"Peg's a very talented seamstress, Mungo. She's entitled to her own life."

"Oh, right." Mungo popped his knuckles to keep busy. "I bet you didn't know she quit backstitching for you six months ago. Did you know that?"

Daisy suddenly turned to her cutter. "Mungo, I have a deal for you. How would you like to buy me out of Bunny Business? I can arrange the loan at my rate. It doesn't matter what you pay."

"What!"

"Daisy!" Teddy grabbed her sister's arm. "Daisy, you can't sell Bunny Business. You're doing a great job."

Daisy closed her lovely brown eyes. "Leo was right. Bunnies is an ludicrous concept. It panders to a fatuous sensibility."

Mungo screwed up his face. "What'd she say?"

"Nothing. She's just upset."

"Wait." Daisy turned to Mungo. "I have a better idea: I

can carry the loan, all I need from you is fifteen thousand dollars a quarter.''

Mungo crossed his arms, tickled pink. ''Miss Daisy, I can't be thinking up all those cute little critters. I can barely keep up with their cute little names.''

''Daisy,'' Teddy stepped deliberately into in her sister's vision. ''You can't talk about this right now. You have to wait 'til you feel better.'' The kettle whistled and she turned to pour hot water into the French press. They were silent for a moment as Teddy filled their cups, and she asked, ''Mungo, how do you take your coffee?''

''Black—whoa, where's she going?''

''What?''

A yellow streak disappeared into the front hall. Teddy clattered down the kettle and dashed after Mungo to follow Daisy. Daisy was already coming back from the living room, holding a pair of shears and Arthur Rabbitstein's fuzzy snout.

Mungo staggered backward into the kitchen, wrapping his arms around his skinny chest. ''Oh, shit.''

''Daisy,'' gasped Teddy.

''I told you: I don't *want* Bunny Business. It's ludicrous, I'm ludicrous, my clientele is ludicrous.'' Daisy slammed the scissors on the table, and paced the wooden floor. Stopped by the far wall, she turned, and paced back. She paused suddenly in the middle of the room, widened her eyes, then paced again, trying to outwalk whatever it was that chased her. Fixedly she stared out the window and then found Teddy, alarmed. Her eyes gaped wildly. ''Teddy, help. I can't do this.''

Teddy snatched the Xanax, or maybe the Ambien, and worked off the lid. ''Wait. Here. Take some of these. You've got to go back to bed.''

Daisy cupped her hand like a beggar.

Mungo rushed to the sink and filled a glass, poised and ready. Daisy tossed down the pills and gulped water greedily.

''That's the way, Miss Daisy. You just drink it down.''

They watched like executioners.

After a moment Teddy said, "Come on, *cara*, let me help you back to bed." She took Daisy's arm and led her upstairs. Tucking her into scalloped sheets, Teddy picked up her sister's hand and stroked it. Daisy's breathing quieted. Finally her eyelids flitted, and a few minutes later she took her first shuddering breath. Teddy tiptoed across the room, closing the door behind.

Down in the kitchen Mungo sat at the table fingering Arthur Rabbitstein's nose. Teddy sat across from him. "Okay, Mungo, what are you not telling me?"

"That part you got right: *I* certainly ain't telling you."

"Then I'll have to ask you to leave."

"Nope, can't do that. I can always lay low, but Miss Daisy—you saw her—she's going to be right up there in the thick of things and she can't defend herself right now."

"Thick of what, Mungo?"

Again Mungo touched his chest pocket.

"Thick of *what*, Mungo?"

"Okay." Mungo sighed. "Peg has an object that needs to be recovered," he chose his words carefully, "so that something Leo grew can come from a place where it's better if nobody knows it's there."

Teddy leaped up. "You've got the coffee!"

"Oh, sure. Coffee's the easy part."

"Great." Teddy dashed over to the phone. "You have no idea how badly people want that. It's incredibly valuable."

"No!" Mungo leaped up and savagely grabbed her arm.

Teddy stared, wide-eyed.

Mungo instantly pulled away and walked across the room. "Oh, Lordy. I'm sorry. I didn't mean to do that." He walked in a tight circle. "I don't hit women. I don't do that."

"It's okay, Mungo. You stopped yourself."

"No, it's not okay. I don't do that, I don't. It's just that I— you can't call anybody right now. It's too complicated."

Teddy rubbed the muscle of her forearm. "Why not?"

"Because . . . it's possible there might be some illicit activity involved, and it's better if an unnamed party does not get wind of the desirability of Leo's coffee."

"Illicit?"

Mungo pressed his lips together.

"Mungo, I already know that Leo was raising marijuana. Guess what? Nobody cares."

His eyes coaxed her on.

"No, wait. The *two* of you were raising marijuana . . ."

And.

". . . and the R-19 is in the same greenhouse as the marijuana."

Mungo heaved a great sigh of relief. "I personally know nothing of any alleged marijuana activity."

"Oh, that's so stupid! How could Leo have possibly gotten himself mixed up wi—" she stopped. "But the hubcap? Tell me about the hubcap."

Mungo twisted in his chair. "It's . . . very important, too."

"That's *not* good enough." Teddy stalked over and held her hand over the phone.

Mungo leaped, and stopped. With utmost restraint, he took one step backward and stood rigid against the counter. Flatly he recited: "The chrome cutout of Marilyn Monroe on my heirloom Ridley is attached with slot tabs. I keep my greenhouse key under Marilyn's skirt. Leo has the only other key."

"Does Peg know that?"

"Not to my knowledge."

"Does Daisy know?"

"I told her yesterday, after you left the shop, so that she might be predisposed to intervene between Peg and I."

"Oh, shoot." Teddy covered her face. "Mungo, the police are going to find out about your marijuana. The university already knows."

"Negative—for the police, that is a negative. And as for the university, it will always protect its own—Leo taught me that one. Besides, Miss Teddy, what's important at this point is not the vegetable matter itself, only a harvested by-product that needs to be delivered to its new owner." Mungo scowled. "This is Sunday. If you could procure my hubcap with the utmost haste, we can recover *both* materials under question and make sure Daisy is not disturbed by anyone anxious for their product."

She sighed. "Mungo, I need to think about this."

He stepped forward. "Miss Teddy, don't you see? There're going to be some very angry people out there if they don't get their property. As I said, I can always lie low. But we got to get this done for Miss Daisy—for me, too, actually, if you don't mind." He moved in close. His plaid shirt smelled of ironing. "Please," he said, "You've got to help me on this one. I'll bring you back the coffee, too."

"Mungo, wait. Just let me think a minute." She stared at the starched pocket imbedded into his shirt: Mungo did his own ironing. And he was good at it.

He watched the change in her face. "I tell you what, I'll make you a deal. I will take over the administration of Bunny Business for the duration, if you will drive up to Roche Harbor and get my key. If you want, I can sit with Miss Daisy 'til she gets up."

"That won't be necessary, Mungo." Teddy glanced at the clock. "I'm calling some women from church in a little while." She sighed. "Okay. I have to go back to Bellingham anyway to finish grading, so I guess I can make a side trip to Roche Harbor."

"Yes!" Mungo affected a bowler's elbow jerk. "When would you get back here?"

"Monday evening."

He frowned. "It'll have to do. Monday night I'll run out to Index and get both the coffee shrubs and the necessary illicit material."

Teddy blinked. "To where?"

"Index, it's in the mountains on the way up to the ski area. Leo wanted mountain air for acidity in the coffee."

"Index is a town?"

"That's right, Index, Washington. The greenhouse is right behind the town wall." He leaned forward conspiratorially. "But you didn't hear that, did you?"

She smiled sweetly. "Hear what?"

For the first time, Mungo grinned. The sides of his bladed teeth were stained tobacco brown.

"But tell me how this works," she said, "After you pick up the coffee plants you . . . bring them to Seattle, and then what? People have already come here looking for them."

"After I pick up the coffee plants I . . . drop them off at the university and tell them R-19 was at Bunny Business. Leo grew stuff there all the time."

Teddy exhaled. "Okay. But this has to be done quickly."

"Yippee!" Gratefully Mungo picked up his empty coffee mug and put it in the sink. Sliding his hands in his back jeans pockets, he smiled with gleaming eyes. "You will not regret this, Miss Teddy."

"Let's hope not, Mungo."

From the table he scooped up Arthur Rabbitstein's tiny muzzle and examined it professionally. "I could probably cut another nose-jobby for the little dude, stitch it on by hand."

"Oh, could you, Mungo? Arthur's such a beautiful piece."

"Done." Clutching the fuzzy snout, Mungo stalked to the front hall. He spotted Daisy's blue keycase on the table and pried off the Bunny Business key. Holding it aloft, he said, "You will not regret this."

5

Teddy drove to the overlook and surveyed the tidy settlement below. Formerly the company town of McMillan Lime Works, Roche Harbor had once quarried, kilned, and shipped the highest grade quicklime in the world. But after the hillsides were played out, and the equipment grown obsolete, the white clapboard seaport was turned into a privately owned marina with deepwater anchorage, a well-stocked bar, and a bugle-and-cannon taps that satisfied the nautical sensibilities of even the most fastidious Seattle yachties.

Rolling down the hill, she parked her little station wagon in front of the lime kilns with their brass historical plaques. She clambered out of the car and buttoned her coat against the westerly. Out on the former shipping wharf—big as a basketball court—was an old-time clapboard grocery: *Closed.* Nearby stood the gabled white mansion of the former lime magnate John S. McMillan—Freemason, friend of Teddy Roosevelt, and a bully Republican in his own right. McMillan's house had been turned into a restaurant, and it, too, was darkened and shuttered on this cold March afternoon.

Turning up her collar, she walked past the marina docks to a third building, the clapboard hotel where McMillan had housed salesmen and guests. Built on top of an old Hudson Bay trading post, Hotel de Haro featured hundred-year-old ivy trunks holding up the balcony and Teddy Roosevelt's flamboyant signature in a register under glass.

The hotel door was unlocked, and she walked across the low-ceiling lobby then tapped the chrome bell on the desk. Nothing happened.

She called up the stairs. "Hello?"

"Hello," called a voice from the second floor. A college girl bounded down the stairs and grabbed a log post to stop her forward progress. She was healthy and bright with a smile like last year's homecoming queen. "Hotel's not really operating now."

"I'm looking for a woman who left your phone number as the place she takes her calls." Teddy pointed to the phone.

"Who's that?"

"Her name is Peg Henley. She just moved up from Seattle yesterday. Heavy-set, Southern accent . . ."

"Oh." The girl looked out to the docks. "She's boat-sitting for the Pattons while they're in Hawaii. *Jamboree*, berth sixteen. There's another woman, too . . ."

"Muriel."

"Yes." The girl craned her neck. "But I don't think they're there right now."

Teddy looked out to read boat sterns; she could not see *Jamboree*. She turned. "Do you know when they'll be back?"

"Couldn't tell you." The girl glanced at the antique telegraph clock, its brass pendulum tarnished the color of tea. "They said they had to go over to Victoria to pick up a sewing machine." From under the counter she pulled out Sasha Bunny, resplendent in gob hat and perfect wool sailor suit. "Look what they make. They're going to sell them in the store this summer."

Teddy bit her lip. "Isn't that sensational work?"

The clerk displayed the pink silk inside of Sasha's furry ears. "They said you need a professional machine to do this because you can't make money under one thousand stitches a minute. Home machines only go three hundred.''

"I think I've heard that someplace.'' Teddy picked up a pen on the desk. "Listen, could you have Peg and Muriel give me a call when they get back tonight? It's fairly urgent.''

"Oh, it won't be tonight. Their machine wasn't going to be ready until first thing Monday morning.''

"Oh.'' Teddy touched the telephone on the desk. "Is this the only phone?''

"Actually we'd prefer they not take calls here. Pay phones are next to the showers . . .''

Teddy scribbled again. "Okay. When they get in tomorrow, please ask them to call me. I'm up in Bellingham, and they can call collect. And I'll try calling them, too.''

"Bellingham.'' The girl looked at the notepad and then at the clock. "If you want to make the 6:40 ferry, you have to leave *right* now. Otherwise it's the 7:50.''

Teddy stroked Sasha's fuzzy cheek. "Then I guess I'd better go.''

Back home at her condo the message light was flashing on the phone. Three calls. Teddy punched "play" and the phone chirped A-flat.

"*Liebchen.*'' Aurie. "I thought you'd be home by now. I stopped by Daisy's around three and Irene Oliveri was feeding her some very tasty-looking lamb chops. A cop came by to clarify some things, but I don't think we were much help. Daisy and Irene were going to take a walk later on, then go to evening church. I talked to Daisy's doc and he'd like to see her tomorrow at his office, so we scheduled the cops again for Tuesday. Irene Oliveri is providing excellent care, but we both agreed we were glad you'd be back tomorrow night . . .

"Can't think of anything else to say, except that I love you more than cartilage.'' He paused. "And I'm not kidding about that.''

The phone chirped again.

"Teddy? This is Daisy. A policeman came by and asked

for Leo's keys. He was *very* nice, he'd make a good bunny."
There was a muffled sound as Daisy fumbled the receiver.
"Please come back as soon as you can, there's something I
need to tell you. Also—Mrs. Oliveri gave me sour cream."

"Oh, dear." Daisy was lactose intolerant, dairy products
ran right through her.

The machine chirped again. "Miss Teddy? This is Mungo.
Listen, something's come up and I have to split town. I sent
some friends up your way, and you'll be fine, just fine—just
do what they say. They need to get their seed material from
the greenhouse and I have their assurance that they will only
take what's theirs and not disturb the coffee plants.

"Sorry to bail out like this, but things'll work out fine now
that you have the key. Best thing to do is, go right now and
make yourself a copy before they get there. You got it?"

"Oh, shit."

"Remember: the greenhouse is on the first road behind the
town wall in the place we were talking about. Green Quonset
hut aways up on the right, can't miss it. I'm real sorry about
this, but I got some friends in Stockton I'm gonna go see.
You take care, now, ya hear?"

The phone chirped a final time and Teddy erased the mes-
sages.

Shoving cold spaghetti into the microwave, she punched in
three minutes and ran upstairs to put on sweats. By the time
the oven beeped she was counting the number of exam booklets on her desk and multiplying by four—the number of essays each student had written. At twenty-two students, that
was eighty-eight essays and—she punched her calculator—at
seven minutes per essay she would finish by—five A.M. Too
little sleep. She punched in five minutes per essay and saw
that she could hit the rack by two.

Pulling out the desk chair, she sat down—fork in hand—
to learn yet more startling new facts about the American
West: how the American "Lois N. Clark" led an expedition
across the continent to become the first white woman to see

the Pacific; how English explorer Captain Hook was killed in the Sandwich Islands, later called Hawaii.

After an hour she got up to do caffeine, and as the teabag leaked into the hot water, she pulled out a road atlas and saw that Index, Washington—population 140—was in the Cascade mountains between Bellingham and Seattle and that Rand-McNally had sprinkled the entire route with green dots: Index was an alpine fairyland. And if the tiny population was an indication of size, the town wall shouldn't be too hard to find.

Cuddling her tea mug, she dove again into the essays. A while later she heard murmuring out on the stoop. She held her breath and listened. There was silence, then a knock at the door. Scooting back her chair, she padded out to the front hall and turned on the porch light.

Through the eyehole she saw two large men with very bad hair. One was ghastly pale, with sunken cheeks and waxen skin. He was wearing a barn jacket—a real one—that had tears on the sleeves and a pinned-on collar. He had faded red hair and a wind-blown gauntness, as if left outside in the Hebrides too many generations.

The faded man blinked with dreadful white lashes, but he deferred to the other. This man had oily black hair and a fixed-from-under gaze like a bull. He paced the porch as if evading gunfire and kept his hands tucked into a black leather motorcycle jacket that had done some serious hard time.

"Wh-who is it?" she called through the door.

The men shuffled on the porch. "We're friends of Leo Faber. Your brother-in-law."

"Leo's dead." She waited.

"Yeah. That's why were here. We're his business partners. Do you mind opening the door?"

She clenched her fists. "I can't do that."

"We just need to ask you something," Black Leather did the talking, his voice bright and earnest. "It'll only take a minute of your time."

"We're even willing to barter," the other added.

The porch light went on next door.

"Go away," she huffed. "Or I'll call the police."

Black Leather lowered his voice. "No, you won't. The ditz is your sister, right?"

Teddy gasped. "I don't know what you mean."

Black Leather shuffled close to the door. "Yeah, well you tell Rabbit Lady we want the seeds, or we want our money back. All of it."

Barn Jacket kibitzed, "Yeah, we're still the only ones can use the product. Tell her *we* got the clients. She don't."

"I just told you, I don't know what you mean." Bravely Teddy peeked through the eyehole. The men shuffled impatiently. Finally one said, "Just give us the key."

"I don't have it. And I don't know where it is."

They banged on the door. "Open up!"

"If I had it, I'd give it to you, I swear. I don't have it. I don't have it!"

The banging was terrible. Her phone rang. "That's my neighbor! I'm calling the police." She darted back to the kitchen and snatched the receiver. "Hello?"

The caller apologized for his wrong number so late at night. He hung up, but Teddy stayed on, listening to the dial tone for a long, long time.

6

Teddy woke icy cold, bathroom tiles inches from her face. Leaping up, she checked her watch. 8:04 A.M. She trounced over the loose sofa cushions and unlocked the bathroom door, behind which she had bolted herself in order to sleep.

Pulling back the upstairs curtain, she peeped outside. The condo landscaping stretched emerald and serene, the dewy lawns their perfect, professional selves. She craned her neck: there were no unknown cars in the cul-de-sac.

She showered and dashed out with her exams, running the car through the latte drive-up on her way to school. Parking in the empty faculty lot, she bounded up to the history department to find it quiet as tree mold. Her colleagues would be sprinting in later, minutes before the noon deadline, only to dash off again, to Bellagio or Berkeley, before the chairman could assign next quarter's committee work.

The exam booklets she plopped into a plastic crate outside her door. A copy of the grades she slid into the secretary's box. Bouncing back down to the parking lot, she drove south on the interstate and turned west for the island ferry. She drove to Anacortes in zero traffic. On-loading was not a problem mid–Monday morning.

The ferry trip, as usual, was splendid. Handel would have done the score. The eastern range of mountains was socked in by cumulus, but to the west the woolly islands were appliqued like piecework, cut from navy flannel and stitched in cotton mist.

Teddy stood on the deck watching seagulls catch Ritz crackers tossed up by tourists, while off the stern the frothy wake splayed in a train of Battenburg lace, much like the one Blossom Bunny wore the time she married Peterkins.

When the purser announced "San Juan Island" through the loudspeaker, Teddy dashed down to the car deck and drove off, heading north toward Roche Harbor. It was 11:10 A.M.

Parking in the Roche Harbor lot, she padded down the dock to find the *Jamboree*.

The boat was a forty-five-foot Bayliner with a boxy salon and sumptuous upper bridge. On the stern under the gilt word *Jamboree* was *Juneau*, her home port. Lights glowed behind the salon curtains and Teddy knocked on the thick bulkhead. "Hello?"

A hugely obese woman slid back the cabin door. "What can I do for you?" It was Peg Henley, carrying at least a hundred pounds more than when Teddy had seen her last.

Teddy blinked. Peg wore a purple Huskies sweatshirt and an impossible bowl haircut—short, with spit curls mounded on her cheeks. Under her knit slacks her belly hung like an ostomy bag.

"Peg?" said Teddy. "I'm Daisy Faber's sister. I left a message yesterday."

"Oh." Peg grabbed the doorframe with a hand blown up by a bicycle pump. "I didn't recognize your name."

"Teddy Morelli."

"Yeah." Peg came out, closing the cabin door behind her. "Did they catch the woman that killed him?"

"I haven't heard yet. May I come aboard?"

Peg looked at Teddy's shoes. They were her wing tips with thick vibram soles. "Could you take those off? They make terrible marks on the deck."

Teddy slipped off her shoes and carried them across to the

salon door. Inside was a sewing shop, neck deep in ribboned trim, bolts of material, and plastic templates straight off the wall of Bunny Business. Across the room Muriel sat behind a computerized Singer barely looking up from her work. Hanging from the bulkhead were old celebrities from Bunny Business: Proud Mary, Peterkins in three sizes, and Bookshelf Bunny, who perched uncannily on the edge of things by virtue of his hardwood torso.

"I recognize these folks," she said.

"They're ours," Peg blurted. "We make 'em in acrylic with cuter ears." She held up a dun-colored Peterkins with ears like dreadlocks. "We've changed the design all around."

Angry color rose in Teddy's cheeks. She turned away, and finally replied, "That's cute as can be."

Muriel rolled her eyes. Positioning the tip of a red ribbon under her needle, she tossed the rest of the hank over her shoulder so it would feed smoothly as she pulled.

"What do you want?" asked Peg. "We don't know anything about Leo, except what Mungo said on the phone."

"Mungo called you?"

She frowned. "He left a message same as you. He said Leo's girlfriend stabbed him Saturday night and now he needs the hubcap back. He's not shitting about the girlfriend, is he?"

"No." Teddy shook her head.

"I thought for sure you were going to tell me Mungo did it."

"Mungo?"

Peg snipped lengths of yellow ribbon, measuring exactly one yard between her stretched-out fingertips and her nose. "Mungo's so gaw-gaw over your sister, he'd blow up the Kingdome, she asked him. I thought maybe he needed to sell the hubcap and split."

Teddy curled her stockinged toes to keep them warm. "Actually, that's what I'm here for. Mungo asked if I would stop by and pick up the hubcap for him."

"You?" Peg looked as if she'd heard Mungo was Arch-bishop of Canterbury. "If that don't beat all." Her cheeks quivered. "Wait a minute, what's Mungo got on you?"

"Nothing." Teddy shrugged. "He's just a friend."

"Did you hear that, Muriel? He's her friend."

"I heard it."

Peg measured ribbon as she talked. "First of all, I guess Mungo didn't mention that the hubcap is mine."

"Aah . . . he said it was his."

"Took my money to buy it, never paid me back."

"Pond scum," added Muriel.

"And secondly, he's so stupid, he don't even know he got ripped off when he bought it."

Teddy shook her head. "No, it's very valuable, as hubcaps go."

"Right." Reaching into the teak-trimmed bulkhead, Peg pulled out a battered two-color catalog. Flipping to a well-worn page, she pointed to a fuzzy black-and-white reproduc-tion of a hubcap on a page of fuzzy black-and-white reproductions. Teddy squinted. Depicted in a dark circle was a pale, smashed-in sombrero with female legs: "Marilyn Monroe on Airvent, Mint: $2,500 to $3,000. Very Fine: $2,200, Fine: $1,000."

Teddy nodded. "Yes. Mungo says yours is mint."

"And Mungo's an asshole." Peg slapped the catalog closed and picked up her scissors again. "Saturday morning I took the 'cap over to a shop on Aurora and the guy showed me a real Ridley's, he's got the '63 JFK. Ours isn't even a Ridley's to begin with."

"It's not?"

"It's a Ridley's knockoff, out of Taiwan in the seventies. Real Ridleys are about three times as heavy, and the chrome silhouette is flame-cut and *welded* on—pure through. Ours, the Marilyn is punched out of aluminum and held on slot-and-tab, very chintzy. He says it's not worth the pot metal it's made of."

Teddy watched the nest of yellow grosgrain swell around Peg's feet. "I think Mungo still wants the 'cap back," she said, "It has great sentimental value to him."

"Tell him I threw it overboard."

Muriel snorted.

Peg played to her audience: "Tell him we're using it for a wok."

The women howled.

Teddy waited, biting her lip, "That's too bad." She stood. "Mungo'll be disappointed. I think he plans to send Daisy up here, if I couldn't persuade you." Teddy gestured around the salon. "And I know Daisy would love to see how differently you're doing her designs." She walked to the door and sat down to put on her shoes. "Daisy even mentioned selling bunnies up here herself, at one point."

Peg and Muriel glanced at one another and Peg finally said, "Hey, listen, we were only kidding. If you really want the hubcap, it's in the trunk of my car."

"Great!" Teddy tied her shoes. "Can we go get it?"

"Only if you tell Mungo I think he's a fool." Peg waddled across the cabin and fished a keychain out of her big tapestry bag. Struggling out the salon door, she heaved herself sideways through the half-gate in the cockpit wall. She panted up the dock, making Teddy pause several times while she looked at objects in the water, readjusted her clothing, made remarks about the sky.

In the parking lot Peg shuffled over to a blue Nissan and sprung the trunk lid. She tugged out a handsome homemade drawstring bag, and held up the black enamel hubcap. The stylized aluminum cutout of St. Marilyn of the Airvent could just as well have been of St. Sebastian and the Arrows. Peg slipped the 'cap back in the bag and handed it to Teddy.

"Thank you," said Teddy. She hugged it to her chest; the well-made bag seemed to give value to the 'cap.

"Wait a second." Peg leaned her weight against the tail lights. The center seam of the knit pants divided her abdomen into two saddlebags. "I usually don't butt into other people's business, but I should tell you, you're better off if you don't buy whatever Mungo's selling, know what I mean? It's like a tapeworm with Mungo—first you think you got rid of it, then you find out it's still in there, sucking away."

"Thank you. I'll try to remember that."

"Yeah." Peg waddled away. "And when you see your sister, tell her I'm real sorry."

Teddy drove up the hill and pulled onto the first gravel road. Sliding the hubcap out of the bag, she shook it back and forth. Nothing happened. She shook again, furiously. An object shifted slightly under Marilyn's skirt. Teddy turned the cap over and saw she would need a pair of pliers to tweak the metal tabs.

Driving to the south end of the island, she parked in the ferry line to save her spot. She trudged up Spring Street in busy Friday Harbor and bought a pair of cheap pliers at the chandlery. Dashing back to the station wagon as the ferry was loading, she drove on, lingering in the driver's seat while everyone else bolted upstairs to the lounges. She pried up the tabs on the 'cap, and tapped her pliers against the rim. A steely high-tech key tumbled into her lap. "Amloy," it read. She clutched the key.

They off-loaded at Anacortes. The giant digital ferry clock glowed 4:40. p.m.

Index, 1 mile.

The sign pointed to a byway so bough-shrouded that evening would fall as soon as she turned. She switched on her blinker and her headlights at the same time.

The beautiful winding lane followed the left bank of the Skykomish River up a walled granite valley. The Skykomish was a mountain stream, white-edged and river-stoned, with the sluiced curves and spinning eddies that urban rafters found pure bliss.

Coming to a steel bridge that crossed over into town, Teddy

turned onto it, only to stop in her tracks. The bridge was one lane wide, and a Budweiser truck was signaling seniority from the other end. Teddy backed up to let him pass. The driver raised a finger in thanks.

She crossed the bridge and stopped abruptly at an intersection. It was the main crossroads of town, or maybe the only one. To the left was a tavern, replete with Michelob neon and Ford-versus-Chevy out front. Across from the tavern was the city park, which showcased an industrial saw blade the size of a Volkswagen. To the right was a tiny grocery, inside which an Asian couple was closing down for the night. Teddy craned her neck to see the cliff behind town. The black granite bluff rose sheer, like something at Yosemite. It was so close to the river it limited human habitation to two streets widths.

Teddy turned right and drove slowly down the pavement, peeking past houses on the river to look for the town wall. All she could see in the dusk was an occasional picket fence. After two blocks town ended. She turned left and left again, driving the "back" street of town, the only other piece of long asphalt. Here, too, she found lush yards and homey cottages, high woodpiles and an old inn—but nothing remotely resembling a town wall.

She stopped at the city park and got out, just in case the town wall was hidden deep in the landscaping.

Standing under the awning protecting the saw blade, she read by the light of a buzzing streetlamp about how this huge toothed platter had once ripped granite from the neighboring cliffs. A thumping noise interrupted her reading.

In the lighted tavern across the street the Ford-versus-Chevy crowd was signaling for her to come on over and have a brewski. She waved cheerfully, and climbed into the station wagon, locking the doors. "Damn you, Mungo."

Again she drove slowly the four blocks of town: there was *no* town wall in Index. She stopped at the bridge, checking traffic. Behind her a battered American sedan pulled out from a dirt track and followed, its old round headlights a cheery yellow. The car needed a muffler badly.

Teddy turned back onto Highway 2 toward Seattle, and watched in her rearview mirror as the sedan followed. *Reptile Museum, 3 miles.* She drove nervously to the museum and when she arrived at the lot, put on her blinker. Behind her the round yellow headlights did the same.

At the last second, she flipped off her blinker and sped past the reptiles. So did the sedan. It was a very old car, large and from the seventies, a Dodge or Ford or something.

"Damn."

Several miles later, without signaling, she pulled off at the police station in Sultan and sat under the street light. The sedan sped noisily past. In the car were two men; the passenger had luminous white skin. The Sultan police station was closed for the night, but out front was an emergency phone under a blue beacon. She stared into her odometer, remembering the sinking feeling when she'd heard "Rabbit Lady." She could not use the phone. What if Daisy was running the marijuana venture? She certainly had more business sense than Leo . . .

Teddy pulled back on the highway, looking for the Dodge at every parking lot. It was nowhere to be seen. In a while she loosened her grip on the wheel.

She glanced behind, and the Dodge was on her tail. Rolling into the busy town of Monroe, she turned into the Dairy Queen lot. At the pay phone she punched in the number to Aurie's house. Then his office.

"Seattle Orthopedic," cooed a voice.

"May I speak to Aurie Scholl, please?"

"Doctor's at the hospital now. He was called in for surgery. Would you like to leave a message on his voice mail?"

Teddy hesitated. "Yes, please."

"One moment." The phone beeped and Teddy began. "Aurie, help. I'm in Monroe and there are two men following me. I can't go to Daisy's because they'll follow me there, and

I can't go to the police because . . . it might be that Daisy's involved with some illegal vegetable matter, so please erase this message as soon as you get it. I'm coming straight to the hospital to see you, and I'll be there in about an hour and a half, so please don't leave. I'm at a Dairy Queen pay phone and I might have lost the guys. It's probably okay, because I don't think they're the ones who killed L—'' *Beep.* Her time was up.

She hung up the phone. The rusty Dodge was across the street, bathed in pink vapor light. Possibly the car was dark blue.

All the way back to Seattle she watched the round yellow lights in her rearview, sometimes close, sometimes far away. Taking the Madison Street exit, she climbed the hill toward Swedish Hospital and watched the Dodge follow. She pulled up close to the main entrance and scurried in.

A volunteer smiled from behind the information desk.

"I need to page Dr. Scholl, please. He's up on surgery." Teddy eyed the front door, waiting for Leo's "business partners" to come barreling in.

"Would you mind waiting over there?"

She clutched the counter. "I'll stand here, if you don't mind."

The volunteer disappeared and after interminable minutes came back. "Doctor's been given the message."

"Thank you." Teddy watched the woman work.

After a while it was clear the two men weren't coming in. Teddy ventured out to the sea of soft gray couches in the hushed vast waiting room. There she joined all manner of other waiters—knitters, readers, criers, prayers.

After a while the corridor doors flew open and Aurie loped out. He was wearing green scrubs, and his surgical mask hung limply around his neck. He stopped on the carpet fifteen feet away. "Teddy, what is it?"

She dashed over. "You're not finished."

"It's a multiple." He lifted his leg to pull up his scrub

bootie. "Hurry. They're calling my next case."

"Did you get my message?"

"What message?"

Teddy glanced at the hospital volunteer who was ardently ignoring their conversation. "Nothing, call me when you get off, okay?"

"I'll come by. Is Daisy okay?"

"Sure," she said.

"Good." He looked at the clock. "I've got to go."

"See you later."

Out on the street the Dodge had disappeared. Warily, Teddy drove north on Broadway and crossed the Montlake Cut. Driving up the lake to Daisy's, she continually checked the rearview mirror, circling Daisy's block and waiting. The Dodge was not there.

Finally she pulled into the drive. Next to her was a sumptuous maroon sedan she'd never seen before. She tugged out her overnight bag, and let herself in the house. It smelled gloriously of garlic. From the sunroom came the sound of TV and the blessed shriek of children. The house had been transformed, it was nothing like the dismal morgue she'd left thirty-six hours before.

"Hello?"

She walked back to the sunroom and stopped in the doorway. The room was colonized by a happy dark-haired family—children, mother, father, and knitting grandmother—all wondering who the hell had just walked into their house.

7

Teddy stood in the doorway of the sunroom. A smiling woman glided over with a baby on her hip. "You're the sister," she said.

"Yes," said Teddy, just as she noticed that furniture was missing from the room.

The woman had a tight handsome chignon swept into a net; she swayed like a dancer with the baby. "My name is Camilla Silva, I'm in sodality with your mother. Irene Oliveri asked me to come."

"Of course. How do you do?"

The dapper Latin gentleman disengaged himself from two giggling girls and stood for introductions.

Camilla gestured to them all. "This is my mother Louisa, my daughters Christina and Xaviera, and my husband Renato . . ."

Mr. Silva bowed from the hip. "How do you do."

"Hello."

"And this"—Camilla twisted proudly—"is Rafe."

Rafe was a plump handsome child with russet cheeks. Teddy put out a finger and he grabbed it with tiny sausage fingers. "Hi, Rafe."

Mr. Silva gestured to take the baby. "Camilla, do you want the feijoada out of the oven? Mrs. Faber will be very hungry."

Teddy followed to the kitchen and watched Camilla pull a casserole dish from the oven. "What did you call that? It smells wonderful."

"Feijoada. Black beans, onions, all different meats. Your sister has said she eats no milk or cheese. Is that right?"

"Yes, exactly." Teddy pointed to the ceiling. "How is she?"

Camilla shook her head. "She wouldn't come down for dinner. She said she was waiting for you."

"Oh, dear." Teddy headed for the door.

"I'm glad you're here." Camilla began to set places at the table. "The kitchen will be all right for eating?"

"Fine. She eats here all the time." Teddy dashed up the stairs and rapped on Daisy's door. "Daisy?" She waited, then let herself in.

The room stank of stale sweat and old Joy. Near the foot of the mahogany four-poster, Daisy lay curled in a ball. She was wearing an extravagantly gathered Swiss batiste dressing gown either purchased in Geneva or homemade, Teddy could not tell which. The gown stank badly.

"Daisy?"

Daisy didn't move.

"You have to get up and eat." The rocking chair from the sunroom was over by the window. "The woman downstairs has this bean dish she made, she says there's no dairy in it."

"Teddy, I can't go down, it's too noisy. Just get me a little soup."

"Daisy, she made it specially. She's from church."

Daisy pulled a pillow over her head. "Just soup, please."

Teddy tugged the gown over Daisy's calves. "Sure. We can do that. You want to get up and put on your robe?"

Daisy didn't answer.

Teddy bounded back down to the kitchen and apologized with a crooked smile. "She asked for soup, and she wants to eat upstairs."

"Soup? I don't—wait, I know." Camilla scooped some of

the black beans into a bowl and held them under the tap. Adding a dash of water, she stirred, then added a bit more. She tasted with a clean spoon and passed the salt shaker over the bowl. She carried it across to the microwave and said, "We give her nice soup." She rummaged through the cabinet. "Your sister would like bread, or crackers?"

"Nothing crunchy, I think." Teddy watched the woman make up a tray and listened to the girls in the sunroom use their father for a jungle gym. When the tray was ready Teddy took it upstairs and let herself in. Daisy hadn't moved.

"It looks good, Daisy."

Daisy groaned. "What if the same thing happens as with the lamb chops?"

"There's no dairy in it."

"No, I don't mean that." Daisy dragged herself from the bed, battling gravity. "It's been so long since I've eaten meat that the food made my pills wear off and I wanted to chop off my head."

Fear stunned Teddy. "Daisy, you cannot chop off your head, do you understand me? You'll go to hell!" She led her to the rocking chair and plopped her down.

"How much would it matter?"

"A lot. Okay?" Lugging Leo's nightstand over for a table, Teddy positioned the food directly in front of Daisy and handed her the spoon. She waited.

Daisy held the spoon like a child with a candle and stared at the tray. Casually, Teddy plucked the spoon from Daisy's hand and ladled up soup. Testing it on her own lip, she touched it to her sister's. Automatically, Daisy opened and swallowed, a reflex from babyhood. Teddy shuddered—she was feeding her big sister.

She dipped the spoon in again, avoiding the flecks of meat. "It's good, isn't it?"

Daisy swallowed. "There's no dairy in it."

"I didn't quite get the woman's name?"

"Camilla something. She knows Marmee."

"Camilla," Teddy repeated. She served up a few more swallows then tested: "Daisy, two men came to see me last night and then followed me today. They said they were business partners of Leo's." She spooned soup into Daisy's open mouth.

"Angus." Daisy swallowed. "Keep away from him, he's very scary."

"Is he the one with dark hair?"

"Yes, the other one is Ghost."

"Daisy, they said they wanted 'the seeds.' "

"That's what I wanted to tell you. Just tell Mungo to pick up the seed packets when he goes out to get the coffee plants for Kevin. Leo said everything is packaged now."

"So you do know?"

"About the marijuana? Of course, it's a high-yield dwarf for greenhouses in Alaska."

"Oh, Daisy!" Teddy dropped her arm to her side, forgetting the spoon. "How on earth did Leo get mixed up in something that dumb?"

"I just told you, Mungo. Mungo fished up there his first season West and when he found out Leo was a botanist, he told him about people in Alaska needing a dwarf for their greenhouses."

"Oh, that is so stupid."

"Teddy, it's not *that* big a deal. Leo enjoyed the challenge." Daisy eyed the spoon at Teddy's side. "And Mungo takes care of the care of the messy parts."

"Well, Mungo's gone to California!"

"Not Mungo!" Pensively, Daisy took the spoon and dipped into the soup. "Did he take Angus's money?" She swallowed. "I don't care, he can have it. But Angus is going to be angry if he doesn't get his seeds. He has to be there pretty soon."

"*There*?"

"Alaska." She swallowed. "Someone else will have to go

to Index and get the seed packets for him. Although I don't think Kevin knows . . ."

"Daisy, I've been to Index. I drove all over town this afternoon. There *is* no greenhouse."

"Yes there is. They go there all the time."

"*Where* in Index?"

"I don't know, Leo never took me. He said I wasn't very good at keeping secrets."

"Oh, Daisy." Teddy sighed. "I'm so glad to hear that."

Far away the doorbell rang and Teddy collected the tray, anxious to see Aurie. "I'll be right back up with your pill. Maybe I can help you wash before you go to bed."

The word "bed" made Daisy remember there was one, and she wandered back to her nest under the duvet.

Teddy balanced the tray on her palm and closed the door behind. Rough male voices floated up the stairs. She froze in place, holding her breath and listening. Cold outdoor air funneled up like chaos.

Camilla's husband was talking in his earnest melodic way, calming whomever was at the door. "I am so sorry," he said. "Mrs. Faber and her sister are indisposed."

Teddy peeked over the railing. The back of the husband's wool trousers was all she could see.

Husband continued, "I cannot allow you to see Mrs. Faber now. Perhaps if you will come back some other time."

"It's only gonna take a moment of her valuable time." It was Angus, and he was trying to affect polite speech. "We only have one item of information to ask her."

Teddy stepped back and waited. For some reason, she knew the husband would prevail.

"Please," urged Husband. "I cannot allow it. You must go."

"But it's highly critical that we discuss a matter of interest with the ladies." In a few more exchanges, Angus wouldn't be able to keep up.

"I'm sorry, Mrs. Faber is under a doctor's care."

The men argued—Angus on the verge of threats—for several minutes, and Teddy stood listening as the clever, courteous Hispanic kept pulling the conversation back to accommodation and good-feeling. It was a masterful performance, one she could not have given herself.

"Okay." Angus was rabid. "But tell her we're going to call."

"I will be happy to convey the message." Camilla's husband clicked his heels, urging the men toward the door.

The door closed and Teddy exhaled as the menace left the house. Arranging an expression of innocence, she carried the tray downstairs and slid it onto the kitchen counter. "Who was that at the door?"

Camilla's husband glowered. "Some riff-raff who say they have business with your sister. I did not know what the trouble was, so I told them to go away."

"That's good. She wouldn't be able to handle visitors right now."

"But, my dear." Silva leaned across the counter. "You now have me worried about your sister. If you wish, I can help you protect whatever it is the riff-raff is so after."

"Thank you." Teddy scooped up the Ambien vial. "But we're so stupid we don't even know where it is." She cocked her head. "You haven't given Daisy her pill yet, have you?""

"No, Camilla was waiting for you."

Teddy brought the Ambien up to Daisy's room and let herself in. "How about a nice bath before bedtime, Daisy?"

Daisy looked through the door at the bewildering array of porcelain fixtures.

"Never mind," said Teddy. "Let's just do your teeth."

"Teeth."

Teddy led her into the bathroom and squeezed toothpaste onto the wetted brush. Daisy rubbed the brush around twice and then became distracted by the running tap. Teddy took the brush away and offered Ambien and a cup of water. Then she took Daisy back to bed, and tucked her in.

"Good night, *cara*. I'll be sleeping across the hall tonight if you need anything." Teddy turned off the light.

"Good night, Teddy. Thanks for everything."

Teddy glowed.

Down in the kitchen Camilla was cleaning up, getting ready to leave. The little girls were in the living room, raucously making Rafe "play" the piano. It was provocative behavior, right on the edge, saying that they were tired of being polite in a strange house. Camilla scraped the remains of black beans into a plastic container and squished on the lid. She smiled at Teddy. "Your feijoada is in the microwave—two minutes, I think. I also saved you some for tomorrow."

"Thank you so much, Camilla. Could you tell me your last name again?"

Camilla smiled. "Silva."

"And your husband is?"

"Renato."

"Camilla and Renato Silva."

"That's right. And the children are Christina, Xaviera—"

"—and Rafe."

The doorbell rang and Teddy glanced into the front hall to see Aurie through the etched glass. She leaned against the counter to contain her pleasure, while from the living room, Mr. Silva rushed to answer the door. She continued, "Did Daisy do anything I should know about?"

"Nothing. I'm sorry we drove her to her room." Camilla collected her utensils from the drying rack and rolled them in a blue linen cloth.

"She seems stable now."

Aurie entered the kitchen and spotted Camilla with her back turned. Kissing Teddy on the mouth, he brushed her backside accidentally and she nearly fell over with desire. He pulled away instantly, as surprised as she was. "Greetings."

Knowingly, Mrs. Silva turned around, smiling. "What time

should I come tomorrow?'' She scooped up her pots and casseroles.

Teddy grimaced as the children smashed piano keys.

"Oh," laughed Mrs. Silva. "Tomorrow only Renato comes with me, he is my driver. I brought the children today because I thought they would cheer your sister. Tomorrow they stay home."

Teddy brightened. "Well, then, how about tomorrow afternoon? I need to go water my mother's plants, and I could also run out and get some groceries for Daisy."

Camilla wrinkled her brow. "They said there is a police interview at two o'clock?"

"Oh, I forgot." The world imploded. Rabbit Lady. Teddy gestured in the air, consciously holding her composure. "How about tomorrow morning? Ten?"

"Fine. fine. I'll see you at ten o'clock." Cradling her dishes, Camilla walked to the front hall. "Girls? Mamma? It's time to go. Where's your father?"

Teddy followed her to the door and watched as the family collected. "Good night, Camilla. Good night, Silvas. Thank you very much."

As the Silva family backed down the driveway, Aurie hung his bomber jacket over the hall chair. "Well?" he said.

"Well, what?"

"What in Fido's name were you doing out in Monroe, Washington this afternoon?"

"You got my message."

"Yes." His eyes flared behind his glasses. "And now I have to go back to the office tonight and erase because I don't know how to erase by remote, so *please* don't leave that kind of message anymore."

"I'm sorry." She turned away and punched two minutes into the microwave. "Can't you erase it tomorrow?"

"No. Mary Lou transcribes from it first thing in the morning. Teddy, my staff can't know that I associate with people who grow marijuana. That kind of stuff gets back to the hospital, do you understand?'' He watched the lighted food go round on the microwave carousel. ''What happened to the men who were following you?''

''It's okay, they came here but they left.''

''No, Teddy, it's not okay. How do you know these guys didn't kill Leo for his marijuana?''

''Because Molly Thistle killed him. Anyway, they wouldn't be hanging around like this if they did.''

Aurie took off his glasses and rubbed his eyes. ''Teddy, next time they come here, you call the police, do you understand? It's the way you protect yourself.''

''I can't! They called Daisy 'Rabbit Lady'; they'll get her in trouble.''

''Rabbit Lady?''

''Aurie.'' She turned away. ''It's under control, okay? All I have to do is give the greenhouse key to the two guys after I get the coffee. That's all they want, then they'll go away.''

''Oh, Teddy.'' Aurie leaned against the counter, rolling his head in lazy circles to work off his ''surgery'' neck. ''Have the police arrested Molly Thistle yet?''

The microwave beeped, she pulled out her food. It was still cold in the center. ''I haven't heard. Did they tell you Sunday why she did it?''

''They didn't mention her at all. It's not a good sign if she's still at large.''

''I think it always takes a few days to collect evidence.''

''Or else''—he glanced at the ceiling without meaning to—''they think there's another person of interest, and they're waiting for that shoe to drop.''

''Aurie, stop it,'' Teddy snapped. ''Daisy didn't kill her husband. And if''—the microwave beeped a second time and she removed her food—''and if she can just get through the part about the marijuana for the police interview tomorrow, everything'll be fine.''

Teddy tested her feijoada. It was seriously Betty Crocker,

savory and home-cooked; Camilla spent as much time on the
sauté as Marmee did on hers.

"Well, if Daisy is so lily-white innocent here, why aren't
you telling the cops about the two creeps?"

"Because." She swallowed. "Because the cops will start
in on her about the marijuana. And she can't handle that right
now." Teddy poured herself water from the tap and sat at the
table.

"So let me get this straight." Aurie joined her. "Molly
Thistle killed Leo, and now two random goons want Leo's
marijuana seeds. What if Molly Thistle works for the goons?"

"Because she doesn't. Because she was so angry when she
killed him."

"You don't know that."

"Aurie, you saw those stab wounds. Those were *not* about
a business deal. Those were from somebody who had had it
up to here with Leo."

Aurie searched her face. "You didn't like Leo very much,
did you?"

Teddy shrugged. "He was okay."

"Did Daisy like him?"

"Of course. He was her husband."

Aurie pushed his glasses up his nose. "Those two thoughts
are not necessarily conjoined."

Teddy swallowed. "You're just cynical because your mar-
riage was such a disaster."

Aurie sat knitting his fingers together. Finally he exhaled,
jerking his hands apart. "So. What are you going to do tomorrow?"

Teddy held up four fingers. "Buy groceries, water plants,
get Daisy through the police interview, then run out to Index
and get the coffee. This time I'll ask somebody where the
town wall is." She suddenly stared at the frosty tabletop.

"What's the matter?" he asked.

She brought her plate to the sink. "Somehow, after I come

back from Index I have to get the key to Angus so he can get his marijuana seeds and stop bothering Daisy. Only thing is, I don't know where to find him.''

"I wouldn't worry about it. It sounds like Angus is pretty good at finding you." Aurie twisted in his chair. "But would you do something for me if I asked?"

"What?"

"Could you wait until Thursday to go to Index so I can go with you? I would much prefer that you don't go out there alone."

"Can't." She shook her head. "But, thank you. I have to get the coffee back as soon as possible. If the cops find the greenhouse first, Daisy could get be in big trouble with the marijuana."

"But you just said she wasn't guilty."

"She's *not*."

"Teddy, you're not listening to yourself. I know she's your sister and it's hard for you to think anything bad abou—"

"Daisy did *not* kill her husband."

He pushed his glasses up his nose, his eyes hard as amber. "Sit down, I want to tell you something. You need to understand."

"Don't patronize me."

"Please sit down." He waited, then quietly started again. "Remember the other night when I came running down the driveway and stopped myself against the hood of the Mercedes?"

Teddy looked away.

"Daisy's car tires hadn't just been rolled the wrong direction, the car had been used. Someone had actually been driving around in the Mercedes."

"No, they hadn't."

"Teddy, look at me. Look." Aurie held up his palms as if feeling the warmth of a fire. "Daisy's car hood was hot when

I touched it. Do you understand what I'm saying? She was out in the Mercedes when Leo was stabbed.''

Teddy leaped up and stared across the lake, searching for bearings in the yellow lights of Kirkland. ''Aurie, you'll have to go, I can't listen to this.''

8

By nine o'clock Tuesday morning Daisy had been washed, blow-dried, and fed. The day was unsettled in a Seattle sort of way—silver with a chance of navy—and Teddy tuned in a quiet FM station to calm them both. Sitting Daisy in front of the radio, Teddy spent a long time combing and curling her hair.

At nine-thirty they took a walk down the hill and became engrossed in the yellow exuberance of the daffodils. They looked up surprised to see Mr. and Mrs. Silva in the maroon sedan. Mrs. Silva rolled down the window. "Good morning. Are you ready for us this morning?"

"Good morning! Yes, we'll be right up. Let me give you the key." She fumbled with her bulky key fob, too tight now that she had added Daisy's housekey and Mungo's "Amloy."

She and Daisy walked home slowly, arriving to the smell of raw onions and garlic. Settling Daisy upstairs, Teddy came down and was overwhelmed by the exotic plenitude spilling across the counters—chilies, limes, kale, whole crab, hot-house tomatoes, green peppers, parsley, onions, a hank of herbs. Mrs. Silva was lining the bottom of a fluted colander with a design of sliced eggs, olives, and shrimp. More vegetables and meats stood ready to be packed in. When the dish was steamed and turned out on a platter, it would be both spectacular and incredibly heavy.

Teddy stood at the counter, trying to quiet her strangely beating heart. "I hope you're not insulted if Daisy doesn't eat very much."

Mrs. Silva smiled. Her skin was rich olive, her chignon plump and tidy under a black silk net. "For her upstairs I make crab frigideira. It's very delicious. For us I make this lot of food because it's better to have a 'house full' than a 'house empty' at this time, don't you think?" Her smile was a balm.

"I think you're right."

"But not full of children."

Teddy laughed, surprising herself. Mr. Silva came in from the sunroom. "What is this?" he said playfully. "No laughing. This is a serious time."

"It is a serious time, isn't it? I wish I could think of a way to make it better for Daisy."

The couple regarded her with suffusing kindness, and she continued, "Or, tell me, is it just going to be a matter of letting days go by while Daisy develops some scar tissue?"

Camilla turned to the counter, and Mr. Silva saw he was left to answer. "Your sister's is not a simple case, I think. Longer than the death for her will be the betrayal. It is such devastation for the trusting soul. Camilla, I am thinking of the poem from Camões: the false knight and the maiden?"

Camilla brightened. "*Falso cavaleiro ingrato* . . . I don't know English . . . ingrato."

Murmuring and translating, they remembered into each other's eyes. Finally Mr. Silva turned to Teddy:

> " '*Tis an old trick to betray innocence.*
> *An honest face, but a heart that stays remote.*
> *. . . when I moan that you destroy me,*
> *you turn and say it is I who maltreat you.*"

Teddy smiled. "That's really good, what's it from?"

"A lyric by Luis de Camões, author of *The Lusiadad.*"

"You're Portuguese!"

He nodded modestly. "I *teach* Portuguese."

"At the U?"

His face clouded. "I've put my application in at many places."

"It's hard to get on, isn't it?"

He nodded wistfully. "When I came to America, I had the idea of returning home a hero, a great success for my country. But—" He shook his head. "There is so much difficulty."

"I'm sorry to hear that, I hope things work out for you."

"Thank you, my dear."

Teddy went to the closet and put on her velvet trenchcoat. "I'm going over to my mother's to water plants, then shopping at University Village. Is there anything I can get for you?"

Camilla surveyed the counters. "Thank you, I have everything I need. You've told your sister you're going?"

"Yes."

"Then we will just move about down here, to let her know there are people in the house."

Teddy smiled gratefully and trotted out to her car. Driving across the Montlake Cut, she climbed the backside of Capital Hill and turned onto her street near St. Joseph's, world's ugliest concrete Gothic church. Pulling into the cracked driveway of the lumbering "Tudor" she had grown up in, she glanced up at the second floor and saw that Marmee still had not done anything about the peeling window sash. Oddly, on the back porch were two mountain bikes.

The kitchen door was unlocked and she walked in. Her baby brother Carlo came rushing from the dining room. "Teddy! What are you doing here?" He tossed his brown ponytail off his shoulder, and she tried not to look at the garnet stud in his nose.

"I'm watering the plants." She cocked her ear to the song of the house. "Who's up in the shower?"

"Nobody." He closed his eyes instantly at his own stupidity. "Just a friend."

She knelt in front of the kitchen sink to reach underneath for the watering can. "Good. I'm glad everyone's keeping so clean."

Carlo relaxed, smiling with the brown chipmunk eyes he had kept from infancy. He leaned against the counter as she filled the watering can. "So how's it going over there?"

"I'm just hoping Daisy can hold it together for the police interview this afternoon. Are you staying here, or at the dorm?"

He shrugged. "Little of both."

"No word yet from Marmee?"

"Okay." He exhaled loudly. "Here's the deal." He was tired of explaining. "I called Elderhostel in Boston and they told me to call this place in California. I called the place in California and they had a recording, so I left a message and they called back and left *me* a message, and said all they could do is leave another message at the tour place in Guayaquil."

"Guaya—?"

"Guayaquil, Ecuador, the boats leave from there. So maybe she got the message, maybe she didn't."

As he spoke a sweet-eyed blonde sprang down the back stairs—barefoot, graceful, her hair still wet from the shower. She smiled and sidled up to Carlo, waiting to be introduced. "Hi."

"Hi," said Teddy.

"Teddy, this is my friend Sarah. Sarah, this is my sister Teddy. She teaches history up in Bellingham."

Sarah flashed a young-America smile. "Hi," she said again.

"Sarah and I were going to bike over to Daisy's, except I don't know what I'm supposed to say to her, do you?"

Teddy flooded the saucers of the African violets above the sink. "Just say you're sorry."

"No, like I mean, now that he's dead, are we supposed to

act like he was some kind of a good deal or something?"

"Carlo, stop it!"

"What?" Carlo flushed red. "You know he was world's biggest asshole."

Teddy gritted her teeth. "Carlo, just keep your mouth shut."

"Well, fuck you."

Sarah blinked. Carlo's red-jeweled nostrils flared and he bore down on Teddy, for Sarah's edification. "I guess the sisters-in-law never got treated to his Mr. Anatomy videos, did they? You know all he uses them for is to cream-off."

"Carlo, don't you dare breathe one word of that to Daisy."

"Well, fuck you."

Teddy ignored him, refilling the watering can at the sink and lugging it up to the front landing where the eight-foot *benjamina* reigned like Empress of China. Teddy saturated the black "Zoo-Do" in her pot, and listened as the tree sighed audibly.

Back in the kitchen Carlo and Sarah had disappeared. Teddy put away the can and leaned on the newel post, calling up the back stairs. "Nice meeting you, Sarah. Carlo—keep in touch."

There was no answer.

She drove back across The Cut to University Village and dashed into the grocery store, filling a basket with Daisy food: French cherry jam, dead-ripe pears, pale water crackers. Across the parking lot in Daisy's favorite bakery, she grabbed a number ticket and spied a bobbling red beret—familiar as Marmee's purse. Quietly she padded over and stood in line. "Hello, Mrs. Oliveri."

"Teddy! Precious girl." Gripping Teddy with red leather gloves, Mrs. Oliveri pressed their cheeks together. "How are you doing, doll?"

Teddy lifted the plastic grocery bag. "Coping—more or less. Thank you for sending Camilla Silva over. She's really wonderful."

"I'm so glad. I would have come myself but our little Amy had her hernia operation Monday. Monica's girl."

"Oh, yes. Did that go all right?"

"Perfectly routine." Mrs. Oliveri moved forward in line. "No word from your mother, I take it?"

"Carlo said he called but it sounds like the Galapagos people are independent contractors and are out on their boat." She shrugged. "So we have no idea whether she's received the message."

Mrs. Oliveri stepped forward again. "You have a rash, doll. What's the matter?"

"Oh." Teddy felt the side of her face. It was prickly and warm. "I didn't realize I was so upset. It must be about Daisy's police interview this afternoon."

"It'll be fine, doll. Just give her her Prozac."

"I will, but I hope . . ." Teddy burst out, "Do you think I ought to get her a lawyer?"

Mrs. Oliveri's eyes widened in alarm. "Why, I don't know. Did she do something wrong?"

"No! Nothing. It's just it's so . . . complicated." Teddy searched for a way to change the subject. She spied the deli case of pastas melanges so improbable their grandmothers would have infarcted on the spot. "Daisy's not eating well. I forgot to tell everybody she was lactose intolerant."

"Oh, my Lord, that's right! Those lamb chops were swimming in sour cream. I'm so sorry, I'll bring something plain tonight."

Teddy stumbled forward. "Tonight?"

"Yes. When you judge the dance contest. Louie said to make sure you were free."

"But I can't do that. I completely forgot."

"Sure you can. It'll work out fine." Mrs. Oliveri moved forward and held up her worn-out Visa card in her red-kid hand. Every clerk in the store jerked around, as if hooked like a fish. "I've known Daisy since she was three years old, we get along great. I made her Communion dress, or was that yours?''

Teddy shrugged helplessly. She had hated her Communion dress, a hand-me-down from who-knows-where. Mrs. Oliveri turned to order the seven baguettes and three peasant loaves her family consumed in a day. She turned again to Teddy. "Is seven o'clock all right? Louie says the contest starts at eight."

"Seven is fine," Teddy mumbled. She ordered croissants and a peasant loaf and drove back up the hill. As she unpacked groceries Camilla nodded toward the phone. "There is a message for you. A young man wants to talk to you about some coffee plants."

"Kevin Hyatt?" She dropped the pears.

"Yes, that's it," Camilla discreetly sniffed the peasant bread, divining the quality of the loaf. "I wrote the number. Do you want me to stay for the police?"

"Yes! No! Oh, dear. I have to stop this."

"You're very upset."

Teddy sank onto a kitchen chair, willing herself calm. She picked up the phone receiver. "I'm sure I can handle the police alone, Camilla, if you two can stay through lunch."

"Yes, I'm sure you're right." Camilla tactfully disappeared into the sunroom.

Teddy called Kevin and got no answer. Next she looked up Seattle University information and punched in the number for Louie Oliveri's dorm room. Three baritones sang "Yip, yip, yip, yip, yip, yip, yip, yip, boom, boom, boom, boom, boom, boom, get a job," and at the chirp she announced: "Louie, this is Teddy Morelli. I won't be able to make it to the Miss Asia contest tonight. So if you could find another judge, I'd really appreciate it. I can even recommend some people who know gymnastic scoring, if you can't find anyone yourself. Or maybe you can get by with just two judges." It sounded unwise even as she said it.

"So, please call me back, I'm at Daisy's house . . ." and she recited the number.

Mrs. Silva announced lunch and the three of them convened around the wrought-iron table in the sunroom, feasting on "cuscuz" that was nothing like the Moroccan dish, its homonym. The steamed food in the colander had been turned out on a platter and was as beautiful as a spilled cornucopia. Teddy nibbled shrimp, black olives, hard-boiled eggs, tomatoes, hearts of palm, all swimming in a sea of seasoned cornmeal mush. As she chewed, the muscles in her neck relaxed incrementally.

After lunch she brought a tray up to Daisy. As Daisy fed herself crab omelet, the doorbell rang and a male voice resonated in the lower hall. Listening through the gaps of her own breathing, Teddy could tell the visitor was benign.

She carried the food tray down to find Dean Havenaw waiting in the living room. He smiled with handsome golf-squinting eyes. Mr. Silva had been acting as host and tactfully took the food tray from Teddy, retreating to the kitchen.

"Dr. Morelli?" Havenaw extended a hand. "Good to see you again."

"How are you?"

Havenaw was one of those clueless older men who did the four-finger handshake with women. He settled onto the sofa again. "Professor Silva tells me you teach history up at Rainwater State."

"That's right, Pacific Northwest."

"*Great* little school up there. Good numbers on females." He shook his head. "Don't know how they do it."

She sat down, smiling. Pretty soon his whole generation would retire. "Would you like some coffee?"

"Oh, no, thank you, just had lunch. Listen." He clapped his hands together. "I don't want to bother Mrs. Faber, I know she's under sedation, but, as you know, there's a lot at stake and we need to get moving on this right away."

"This?"

"Yes. I need to state our position. I understand that Mrs. Faber will be keeping the coffee plants until she determines the highest pr—"

"Mrs. Faber doesn't *have* the coffee plants."

Havenaw frowned. "Of course, that's what you've said. But she also needs to know that the coffee is essentially useless at this stage. Who knows, it may never be of value at all, if this keeps up."

"Who knows?"

"Yes, exactly. And from our end, Mrs. Faber needs to understand that—I've been chatting with the board on this, they're behind me one hundred percent—that they suggested it might be appropriate to put out a public notice that the university considers return of Dr. Faber's coffee plants a matter of highest priority. I said I thought that would be a little premature and that we should chat with the family informally to see if they could tell us under what conditions the hybrids might be turned over."

Teddy sighed. "Actually, Dr. Havenaw, you may not believe me, but I am working on that right now. As I said, we do not have them at this time, but I've been given a pretty good idea where to look. And if we can get through the police interview," she looked at her watch, "in a *very* little while, I will go out and get them and return them as quickly as possible."

He stared, uncertain which part to believe. "Good, good." Sinking back into the couch, he crossed his leg, tugging on the honed pleat in his pants. "I'm glad to hear that, because as you probably know, being an academic yourself at such a fine institution, the important part is—I've been chatting with our A.G. and he's absolutely inflexible about this—"

She tried to pay attention.

"—is that the coffee hybrids belong to the university, and not Dr. Faber's estate. So we all feel it's very important that they be returned as quickly as possible so no talk of prosecution needs to come up at all, do you understand?"

"Well, absolutely." Teddy wrinkled her brow. "Although, the other night Leo was talking about patents and all that . . ."

"Oh, yes, yes, yes, yes." He leaned forward, more tête-à-tête. "You can be sure Dr. Faber's estate will be compensated quite handsomely, *if* anything actually comes from the idea—no problem with that. The thing to know is that Mrs. Faber herself may not ever legally get involved in marketing—the A.G. is quite sure about that. ' . . . may not patent, sell, publish or utilize . . .' Terrible restrictions. Airtight.

"So you see, it really is better if your sister bows out gracefully at this time and just takes her compensation, whenever that comes along."

"Well, good." Teddy stood. "I know you and AgroGene are over a barrel about this and I'll tr—"

"No!" Havenaw bolted up, too. "I mean, no, the A.G. is very clear about that, too: AgroGene does *not* own the plants. And since it will probably develop that we find Kevin Hyatt has committed a *grievous* error in judgment, the university has decided it must disengage itself from any further association with AgroGene. We have a moral obligation, you know."

"Kevin?"

Havenaw bit his lip, looking away. "Forget I said anything."

"Kevin?"

"I shouldn't have mentioned it. Kevin is very young and we both know—as educators—that young people can be very impulsive at times. Listen." He twisted around. "Is there a fax machine here? I should send over a copy of the original contract between AgroGene and the university . . ."

"Daisy doesn't have one here."

"Very well." Havenaw took out a soft leather notebook and a fat pen. "I'll get someone to run over here with a copy. You really need to read and understand the documents." Havenaw sat down again.

Teddy had no choice but to follow.

He waited, beaming sympathy and positive regard. "This is a very stressful time for all of us, isn't it?"

"Oh, yes." It was one-forty, the police would be there in twenty minutes.

"And it's very important that we remember our loyalties at a time like this."

Her eyebrow lifted.

"I mean," he said. "Considering the situation we're in, we wouldn't want anybody besides a Pacific Rim sponsor— what am I saying? a *Seattle* sponsor—to take the credit for the first chocolate coffee, now would we?"

"Of course not."

"So. I guess we know where each other stands?"

"A bit, yes."

"Well, then. The next thing I should tell you is that before we actually go public on this, we would like you and Mrs. Faber to know that if either of you happens to remember where the coffee trees are, and can return them to us *in perfect condition*, we would be willing to forget that they were missing, and remunerate with a finder's fee of thirty thousand dollars."

Teddy's mouth fell open.

"Of course"—he searched her face—"the amount is still negotiable . . ." He ended in a plea: ". . . if that's not enough?"

Teddy caught her breath. "No. No. That's fine. I'll tell Daisy."

"Good. Well, that's that." He slapped his knee and stood again, walking to the hall. As he slid into his trenchcoat, Mr. and Mrs. Silva emerged from the kitchen, dishes and shopping bags in hand. Exchanging high courtesies, the three left together.

9

Three officers crowded the porch. Two were in uniform—fine wool long sleeves in smoky blue—and the third in "plain clothes": a man so cropped and buffed he would never be able to work undercover.

Teddy read their nametags as she let them in: tall Officer Emerson with the soft gray eyes, blond Officer Kozak windburned from skiing, and finally, tag-less Officer Plainclothes whose name was only mumbled.

The policemen brought in camera gear and several cardboard boxes, which they set on kitchen counters. Like most visitors, they immediately wandered to the back windows to check the view. Officer Plainclothes began poking a light meter into the air and—delighted with the pearly radiance off the lake—set up a video camera aimed at the kitchen table.

At the counter Officer Emerson pulled out a clipboard from one of his boxes. Wedging it under his arm against his rib cage, he continued to work as if it were not there. He turned to Teddy with eyes like silver frost. "How'd Mrs. Faber do yesterday at the psychiatrist?"

"I don't know, I didn't ask."

Emerson said, "He said he thought she'd be stable on her meds."

"*You* talked to him?"

"I've been assigned to Mrs. Faber full-time. Which reminds me: Tell her they're releasing the body early next week if she wants to do something about a memorial service." He glanced toward the hall. "She ready to see us?"

"I'll go get her." Teddy dashed up to Daisy's room and found her just as she had been left twenty minutes before—combed, clean, sedated, rocking in the chair. Teddy caressed Daisy's hand. "Daisy, the police are here. Can you come talk to them?"

Daisy looked up brightly. "Is this the one who looks like a bunny? Sort of gray and silvery?"

"You'll have to come see yourself." She led Daisy downstairs and back to the kitchen. The cops fell silent.

Officer Emerson pulled back a chair and seated Daisy at the end of the table. As he settled in on her right, Daisy twinkled knowingly, to indicate how well Emerson would make up in mohair velvet.

Officer Kozak sat on Daisy's left, and since no one seemed to care about Teddy, she pulled out a chair down-table, like a uninvited guest.

Officer Plainclothes sauntered in from the living room and murmured to Teddy. "What happened to the big guy out there?" He meant Arthur Rabbitstein.

Teddy murmured back. "Daisy cut off his nose. She's been sort of self-destructive lately."

"Bummer."

Serenely Daisy watched Teddy and Officer Plainclothes huddle. The filtered daylight was soft as powder against her face and she gazed at Officer Emerson's hands. Teddy looked, too. The hands were huge, useful, and ruddy, with injured blue-black nails. They were unlike Aurie's hands, or anyone else's she usually saw.

"Have you arrested Molly Thistle yet?" asked Daisy.

Officer Emerson went on filling out the top of a triplicate form on his clipboard. "Not at this time."

"But you talked to her?"

"I'm not at liberty to disclose information about the case—ma'am."

"But you expect me to answer your awful questions?"

Everyone went silent. At the other end of the table the video camera was already running. Officer Emerson glanced up from his clipboard. "The house number here is 3104?" he asked.

"Yes," mumbled Daisy.

"And the zip is 98108?"

"105."

"Mrs. Faber, we still have a lot of gaps to fill in about Saturday night. First off, we need to *completely* document your movements from the time you left Oliveri Coffee Company until the time your husband's body was found at . . . 12:13. Could you tell us what time you left Oliveri?"

Daisy shook her head. "I can't even remember how I got home. Although I did get here . . ."

"Daisy, you came home with Aurie and me, remember? It was about ten o'clock—I guess."

Beside her Emerson wrote, "2200—Leave Oliveri Coffee with sister Teodora Morelli and . . ."

"Aurelien Scholl." She spelled the name for him.

Emerson glanced at Daisy, "And the three of you arrived here . . ."

Teddy answered, "Fifteen minutes later."

He turned and flared: "We'd like *her* to tell us, please." He turned back to Daisy and was instantly mild. "And after you got home, Mrs. Faber, then what happened?"

"I don't remember," said Daisy.

"Did you go anyplace at that time?"

Daisy shrugged. "I don't remember."

Teddy squeezed her fists under the table. Like a deer catching scent, Officer Emerson turned to her. "And you, Miss Morelli, you and . . . Mr. Scholl. You just hung around the house with Mrs. Faber from 10:15 on?"

"No. Aurie and I took a walk. When we got back, Daisy

had just gotten the phone call from Leo. That's when we drove her over to the university.''

"And how long would you say you were gone?"

"Walking? About an hour and a half . . .''

"Long walk."

"We got lost."

"Lost." He wrote it down. Turning to Daisy again, he asked, "And you didn't go anyplace while they were 'lost'?''

Daisy put her hand over her eyes. "I don't know. Saturday . . . sometimes I go out."

Emerson wrote on his clipboard, then looked at Officer Kozak. "Steve, you want to get the glossies?''

"The bushes?''

"Yeah."

Officer Kozak went to a cardboard box on the counter and pulled out a file folder buckling with eight-by-ten photographs. Diligently keeping them from view, he sorted through, and brought one over to Emerson. Teddy squinted. All she saw was gray dirt and leaves.

Officer Emerson positioned the picture in front of Daisy and used the tip of his pen. "See those marks there, those little Cs'?''

"Yes."

"Those are high-heel prints in the flower bed outside your husband's window."

"Oh," said Teddy. "I can tell you about that. When we were trying to get inside, Daisy ran around to call Leo through the window."

Emerson's eyes flamed like gas jets. "We'd like *her* to tell us, please."

"Sometimes I-I stand in the camellias outside Leo's office when I spy on them."

"And you did that Saturday night?"

"Y-yes. I drove over and looked in, but they weren't there. That's why I drove around looking for them. I couldn't find them, so I came home."

"Miss Thistle states that after the coffee tasting, Dr. Faber drove her directly home, telling her he had work to do at the lab."

Daisy nodded, using an index finger to understand their route. "So he dropped her off in Ballard and then she took a car and followed him back?"

Emerson stared at his pen.

Daisy tried again: "He dropped her off. She came back to his lab and stabbed him."

Emerson clicked his ballpoint. "Mrs. Faber, for the record, Molly Thistle is documented as being dropped off in downtown Ballard by your husband at . . . 10:25."

Daisy added, "And she slipped out later and stabbed him."

He leafed through the clipboard and read. "Molly Thistle was dropped off by Dr. Faber at her apartment above the Kitty Kat Tavern during a replay of the Sonics game at 2225 hours and she stayed downstairs at the Kitty Kat watching a TV movie until . . . three A.M. I have a list of nine witnesses."

Daisy stood. "She's tricked you, don't you see?" She rushed to the window and clutched the sill. When she walked back to the table, it was obvious she could not sit down. She dashed to the counter, grabbed the cookie jar and hugged it— a ceramic cottage with a russet roof and foxglove border.

Teddy padded over. "Daisy?"

"Shut up, Teddy."

Teddy stared.

"Mrs. Faber, the tape is still running." Emerson touched her chair back.

Stiffly Daisy sat down again, this time, pained alertness in her eyes.

"Mrs. Faber, a campus security guard recorded that he used a master key to let your party inside Gilman Greenhouse at 0013 hours Sunday morning. Do you have any comment on this fact?"

"No."

Casually, he flipped a page. "So, typically, when you go

to your husband's office, you use your own key?''

Daisy seethed at his simple-mindedness. ''I don't *have* a key to Leo's office. I never go there without him.''

''In which case, you wouldn't mind surrendering your husband's keys at this time? For testing purposes.''

''I told you Sunday, I don't have Leo's keys.'' She scanned their faces. ''Where are they? Weren't they on his body?''

Emerson scribbled silently.

''Well?'' Daisy's eyes darted from man to man. ''Where are my husband's keys?''

''Thank you, Mrs. Faber. That's all we needed to know.''

Officer Kozak leaned his chair back to look into the front hall. ''Bob,'' he said gently, ''we got an 'at large' and she says the key to her house is missing. We—''

''Right.'' Emerson, too, glanced at the hall. ''Mrs. Faber, since you've indicated your husband's keys are missing, could you please remember to use the bar lock on your front door until you get the deadbolt changed. Can you do that?''

Daisy was confused, Emerson turned to Teddy. ''Can you do that? We recommend you change the locks today.''

''Sure.''

''We're also watching the house for you.'' He scribbled more, then looked at Kozak. ''You wanna . . . ?'' He made clipping motions with his fingers.

Solemnly Kozak walked to the counter and returned with a white paper bag. He laid it in front of Daisy. The bag was fitted with a clear plastic window, and inside was a pair of chrome sewing scissors.

Daisy's lip began to quiver. ''They're the ones, aren't they?''

Kozak smoothed the bag flat for a better view. ''Mrs. Faber, can you identify these?'' The scissors were polished, pointed and small—a lady's size—exactly made for cutting fabric. The pivot screw was crusted scabby brown.

''Those are my old ones,'' Daisy said. ''Leo kept them in his desk.''

"In the bottom left-hand drawer, wasn't it?"

"No," she said curtly. "The center top."

Emerson grunted. He moved the scissors closer. "And these . . . when you found your husband using them to trim a photo Saturday night, you argu—"

"A photo?"

"He was trimming an eight-by-ten picture of himself to make it fit five-by-seven."

"Oh."

"And we would prefer that you not interrupt our questioning." Emerson started again. "So when you found your husband using the scissors to trim a picture, you had an argument and he hit you, so you felt you had no recourse but to defend yourself . . ."

Exasperated, Daisy pushed back her chair and walked again to the window. "Why don't you show them to Molly Thistle?"

"Mrs. Faber, could you sit down again, please?"

Warily Daisy eyed the chair. "Didn't she leave footprints? There was blood all over the place."

The officers glanced at one another and Emerson stood, poised behind Daisy's chair. "Mrs. Faber?"

Daisy sat, and Emerson explained kindly, "Most people O.J. their shoes these days—take them off around blood." He touched his watch as a question to Officer Plainclothes and the cameraman signaled okay. Emerson exhaled. "Okay, Mrs. Faber, only a few more questions and then we'll leave you alone."

Daisy turned. "Teddy, may I have some water, please?"

Teddy leaped up and came back with filtered water from the fridge.

Daisy gulped and set the glass primly on the table. Officer Emerson began again. "Mrs. Faber, there are rumors that your husband may have been involved in the growing of illicit plant material at one time or another, possibly even in your own basement. Do you have any comment on that?"

"None."

"So your husband raised marijuana in the grow room of your basement?"

Daisy aimed her chin. "My husband was a nationally known geneticist, he published in some of the most prestigious journals in the world. In the course of his research he's had contact with over a thousand different plant species at one time or another. If you ever hear rumors about a man like Leo, it's because they're the product of petty and envious minds."

"Yes, ma'am. Thank you. Just one last thing." Emerson looked up. "Steve? Pad?"

Officer Kozak plucked the bagged scissors and the photo glossy from the table and laid out a yellow legal pad and a freshly sharpened No. 2.

"Mrs. Faber, we know this is a delicate subject, and we will try to approach it with sensitivity and discretion," he droned, "but the final thing we need to ask you is to make a list of all the people in Dr. Faber's acquaintance who he would have either let into his office Saturday night, or who could gain entry on their own. We've already spoken to his students and office personnel and we're moving through that, so you needn't name anyone who worked there."

Daisy pushed away the yellow pad. "I'm sorry. I won't do this for you. You'll have to ask Molly Thistle how many other women she shared him with."

"Yes, ma'am. We already have." He pushed the pad back and waited.

Daisy folded her arms.

They waited.

After a bit of silence, Emerson looked at his watch and made the motion to Officer Plainclothes to "cut" the camera. "Thank you, Mrs. Faber. I guess that's it." Emerson's eyes were the minted gray of a conqueror's new coin.

Teddy leaped up and tried to circle Daisy's shoulders. Daisy rose and stumbled, and the two of them retreated to the corner of the room. They watched as the officers packed their equipment, making small talk, pointedly ignoring the fact that they had just shattered what was left of Daisy's life.

With growing fury, Teddy defiantly scooped the pill vials off the refrigerator and led Daisy to the front hall. Calling back from the bottom step, she said, "Could you please let yourselves out and punch the door lock when you leave?" She marveled at her own civility.

The sisters stumbled up the stairs, listening to the front door close below. "I'm sorry, Daisy. I should have gotten you a lawyer. It was my fault."

Daisy broke away, rushing to the windows to gorge her eyes on the snow-covered foothills. "What do I need a lawyer for? Unless it's to help me figure out how she worked her plan . . ."

Teddy tendered cautiously: "But, you know, you said yourself you were out in the car Saturday night. It might be that you don't remem—"

"Oh, stop it, Teddy. I always go out and follow them around." Daisy stared unseeing. "It's *got* to be Thistle, Leo didn't have time for more women than that." She turned, eyes blazing. "The question is, how'd she get away with it?"

Teddy turned away, setting the pill vials on the dresser and pulling back the duvet. The scissors were Daisy's exact size, they would have been so easy to use when Leo turned his back to her. "Daisy, I think you should lie down. Maybe you should take some Ambien."

"I'm not going to take Ambien anymore. I'm going to stand here and think about this. Teddy, you're clever, how did she do it?"

"Daisy, please. You're getting all worked up." And Aurie had known it was Daisy all along. He was just waiting for Teddy to find out.

Daisy paced the room. "I'm *not* worked up. "It's just that sometimes I can't believe Leo and I lived on the same planet. It's hysterical, isn't it? He's off poking that cute little girl who thinks he's Jesus T. Botanist, and here I am, stuffing idiot bunnies in Pioneer Square.''

"Daisy, please don't talk like that." Teddy shook her head to clear it. "Maybe, if we're lucky, this is about Kevin and the coffee plants.''

"Kevin can't steal the coffee plants. They're useless without the patents.''

"Well, what then, the marijuana?''

"Teddy, I told you: the marijuana is nothing, it was just a lark.''

"Well, the police don't think that!" Teddy dropped into the rocking chair. "Actually, I hope it is about the marijuana, since you barely know anything about it.''

"What are you talking about? I know all about the marijuana. I know more than *she* does.''

"Yes, but you said Leo never took you to the greenhouse.''

"So? That doesn't mean anything. I was there from the beginning, when Mungo and Leo did specs on the Alaska dwarf. They even kept the plantlets here at the house.''

"Then how do you know Angus didn't kill him?''

"Because Angus was in awe of Leo. He'd practically genuflect every time he saw him.''

Teddy stood. "Okay. But the important thing here is that you were never involved in the business end of things. All you've done is let them grow plantlets here in the house.''

"Oh, Teddy, stop being so naive." Daisy went over to the dresser and opened her underwear drawer. Reaching beneath a pile of blue panties, she tossed a roll of bills onto the bed. It was the size of a potato.

"Daisy!''

"The first time he gave me money was easy. It was only a thousand dollars so I wrote down that Leah's of Leavenworth bought twelve Kris Kringles instead of eight. But this, I don't know what to do about this. He said just to hide it in the books, but I can't tell if I should lie about inventory too, can you?''

"Daisy, how much is that?"

Peevishly Daisy rubbed her forehead. "I don't know."

Teddy scooped the offensive roll off the bed. It was cinched with a thick blue rubber band gagging the mouth of a big new Ben Franklin. Ben glared accusingly at the sinner who held the roll. "Daisy, you have to do something with this. What if the police come?"

Daisy tucked the money into the pocket of a white terry robe on the door.

Picking up the phone receiver, Teddy sat on the bed.

"Who are you calling?" asked Daisy.

"It's not about the money. I need to make sure Louie Oliveri has a replacement judge for the Miss Asia Pageant tonight. I'm going out to Index to find the greenhouse." She gestured toward the bathrobe. "How about when I pick up the coffee, I leave the money out there? That way, no one can connect it to you." She looked up. "Who do you want to come stay with you tonight?"

"Nobody." Daisy eyes glinted. "I'm going with you."

"No, you're not." Teddy glanced at the pill vials.

"But I have a plan, before we go." Daisy flitted across the room. "I know who can tell us where the greenhouse is. Also who has Leo's keys."

"Molly Thistle?"

Daisy sang, "That's right. If she really did work for Leo like she says, what she did was package seeds at the greenhouse—there should be tons of them now, Mungo's been drying for weeks. And if we can trick Molly into giving us the keys at the same time, that's just like having her admit she killed Leo. Get it?"

"No." Teddy furrowed her brow. "Did she take the keys to sell the coffee herself?"

"Who knows?" Daisy shrugged. "I can't tell you what goes through that girl's brain."

Teddy said nothing. She punched Louie's number and

again listened to Three White Boys sing "Yip, yip, yip, yip, boom, boom, get a job." *Beep*.

"Louie, this is Teddy Morelli. I hope you got my message earlier. As I said, I won't be able to judge the Miss Asia Pageant tonight. Could you please call me at Daisy's and we'll work something out." She recited the number.

She cradled the receiver and Daisy asked, "Well, are we going to Molly Thistle's or not? I'm going to wear my gaucho pants, and my boots."

Teddy glanced again at the brown vials on the dresser and punched the Silva's number into the phone. "Daisy, how about this: how about if you take your pill and go to bed, I'll go over to Ballard and talk to Molly Thistle?"

10

Teddy pulled into the old Scandinavian fishing town of Ballard, one of the few waterfronts in the city that had not been turned over to Starbucks and Flipper. Down at the docks it was almost quitting time, and already shipyard workers were jaywalking to the taverns. Up on Market Street pickups were double-parked, flashing safety lights, and shetland-clad yuppies cliqued in front of chandleries. In every window the merits of Volvo Marine were touted.

A fisherman in gum boots dashed in front of Teddy's car mid-intersection—she jammed on the brakes. Swamped by pedestrians, she glanced down at the fishing fleet docked in Salmon Bay. From a huge open shed blue welding sparks blitzed like fireworks, while all around little yellow forklifts zipped like bumper cars. The money was made in Alaska now. But even Alaska was starting to dry up.

Parking on a brick lane, Teddy got out and followed the bar signs down to the Kitty Kat Tavern. Beer neon glowed in the window and she stood across the street judging its safety—her safety, actually.

The Kitty Kat was a two-story 1890s building, continuously refaced and remodeled, now striped down to its bare facade, ready for the whole process to start over again. It was a troubled place, for serious drinking and serious something else, although Teddy could not tell what. The somber afternoon was nippy and she buttoned her brown velvet trenchcoat and tied the sash.

There were apartments above the Kitty Kat, reached by a metal stairway outside. Climbing the stairs, she entered a stale, moldy hallway and closed the door behind. She sniffed. Upstairs at the Kitty Kat was like stepping back into the Gold Rush. The hall smelled of brittle wallpaper and sun-dried wood, and unlike the front facade of the Kitty Kat, hadn't been touched in a hundred years.

She glanced around. The hallway glowed in sepia tint, with old-growth doors and foot-high fluted moldings. The dense Douglas fir wainscoting was rich as cognac, deep as amber. Mottling its surface were blebs of dark varnish that had cooked off decades ago.

Teddy looked at her shoes, wondering about noise. The floor was ravaged fir, nailed with tin patches, lined with carpet runners. She took a step—and squeaked. Stopping in her tracks, she glanced up at the frosted transoms above the doors. Somewhere down the hall someone was sawing wood. On the first door, she read the card: "Watkinson."

Stepping onto sturdy flooring near the wall, she tiptoed to the second door. She sniffed—it was a janitor's closet. Then she tiptoed to the last door. Behind this door was *not* the sound of sawing wood—it was the sound of a woman feigning pleasure in intercourse, and doing it badly. Teddy turned and tiptoed out.

Down on the street a gust blew up from the channel. She shivered and turned up the collar of her trenchcoat. The gesture caused a wizened fisherman to do a double-take and stare. Teddy realized she did not know the street codes here. As the man waited for more enticement, she lowered her head and walked briskly to the car, locking the door. She waited. The man left the street. Down in the shipyard, the whistle blew quitting time.

Evening gathered in the shadows, and from the car she

couldn't see the Kitty Kat stairway. The best place to wait would be in the tavern, at a table by the window. Shipyard workers swarmed up the hill.

She looked in the rearview mirror. "Oh, right, Morelli, you're going to Happy Hour." She glanced at her velvet trenchcoat and neat gabardine slacks: women's rights to the contrary, she was asking for trouble.

Wrenching the mirror around, she mussed her hair—but that certainly wasn't going to do it; everyone north of Portland had mussed hair. Opening her purse, she rummaged through the makeup bag—lipstick, Chapstick, a tampon from the Ming Dynasty. Prying apart an eye shadow compact, she examined the four tiny squares of color—two buttercream shades worn down to bare metal, two dark tints she never touched. She stroked her finger across the khaki green and rubbed it in the socket under her right eye. She stroked again, and rubbed, trying to remember where the color from a black eye actually belonged. Then she opened the car door for light to admire her work.

In the dusk, she looked like a woman with a Recent Past. She climbed out of the car and walked down the street to the tavern, grabbing a window table before they were all gone.

A waitress approached and Teddy looked up brightly, testing her makeup job. "Whatever you have on draft, please."

The waitress's eyes softened in pity. "Sure, baby. I'll be right back."

Beyond an archway in the rear was a magnificent mahogany bar—carved, mirrored, thirty feet long. Above the bar was a bright square of hockey game, the only light in the room. Loud, witty conversation signaled that Happy Hour had already taken off.

A man craned his neck through the archway to scout for "talent" in the front room. He spotted Teddy, and a moment later another man gawked with him from the arch. Teddy turned full-face, and looked at them inquiringly. Thoroughly put off, they disappeared into the dark.

The waitress returned with her beer.

"That's a sensational bar back there, is it original?"

"Naw, we bought it from another place down the street. Came around the horn before Guadalcanal."

Teddy bit her lip, but blurted anyway: "I think that would be 'around the horn' before the *Panama* Canal, wouldn't it? 1914 or so?"

"Umm."

A pot-bellied policeman sauntered in, making his way to the back room. The noisy revelers shouted insults enthusiastically and, satisfied with his reception, he came out to the main room and fitted himself over the stool in front of the cash register. Here was the real heart of the bar—the waitress's office, where she kept her cigarettes, coffee, and ashtray. In front of the cop a china mug instantly appeared, and he glanced professionally at Teddy. Bravely she showed him her black eye.

He looked away poker-faced and the waitress poured him coffee. "Want to taste something good?" she asked.

"What is it?" He frowned, patting his belly.

Without answering, she turned, busying herself at the warming oven. In a few minutes she spun around proudly, placing a serving bowl of crispy dessert in front of the cop. Teddy could smell it across the room. It was warm and sweet, lacquered with icing glaze. Before the cop could protest, the waitress snatched the whipping cream from the cooler and shook, swirling hogs' ears of calories on top of the sugary breading.

The policeman stared glassy-eyed. "That's . . . really something." The bowl contained enough calories to fuel a power plant.

"Want some ice cream?" asked the waitress.

"No! No thanks." The cop picked up his spoon. "What do you call this?"

"Taste it first."

He dipped in, chewed, carefully swallowed. "Umm,

good.'' He put down his spoon and sipped some coffee. ''What is it?''

The waitress beamed. ''Bread pudding. I make it from day-old doughnuts. What'd ya think?''

He sized up the task ahead of him. ''It's good.''

Teddy watched the poor cop shovel in the delicacy as the fabric of his shirt visibly expanded. On the edge of her vision was movement in the alley. A buoyantly healthy man sprang onto the sidewalk and stopped to zip his blue satin baseball jacket. ''Eterna Life-Caps'' was scripted across the back.

Mr. Life-Caps bounced when he walked; his white running shoes seemed to have a life of their own. Pacing like a boxer, he stuffed his hands in his pockets and glanced down the street. He was a gym rat, no doubt about it, with shoulders like the decks of aircraft carriers and a UV facial glow that wouldn't need a touch-up for another two weeks.

Life-Caps glanced in the Kitty Kat window. Teddy quickly leaned over to check the score of the hockey game. When she looked back, Mr. Life-Caps was gone.

Glancing at her watch, she put three dollars under her beer glass and smiled at the waitress. ''Thank you.'' She walked to the door.

''You take care, now, you hear?''

Teddy slipped into the alley and climbed the metal stairs. Quietly she opened the door and listened. Behind the last door a woman was singing ''Yesterday,'' picking out chords on a rich guitar. She had a sweet voice, but was new to the guitar.

Teddy knocked and the singing ceased. The door opened and Molly Thistle stood clutching the guitar by its neck. She gaped at Teddy's face with repulsion, then recognized the khaki tint for what it was. ''You're the sister.''

''Yes.''

Molly moved aside. ''Come on in.'' She was barefoot and her coppery head wore a halo of tousle. Under her tee-shirt, her full breasts hung braless.

The single-room apartment was set up for art. Chalk

sketches were tacked on the walls and a new hardwood easel stood perpendicular to the windows. The sketches were quite good—of artists' models and bar patrons—but most were only half-finished, or done in profile with lots of shading.

Teddy fished into her purse and wet a tissue with her tongue. Rubbing it in her eye socket, she said, "I had to sit downstairs and this kept people away. You had company."

"Yeah." Molly dropped to the daybed and buffered herself with the guitar. "I was talking to my nutrition counselor about the stress." She glared accusingly. "He says I'm way low on zinc."

"I'm so sorry."

Molly took in Teddy's coat and shoes and precision bangs. She strummed an E-minor. "Does this mean they arrested your sister?"

"No."

"She knows it was part her fault, don't she? Way she does doormat for him. What you gotta do with people like Leo is bully back. They're so full of themselves, they don't even notice."

Teddy narrowed her eyes. "Daisy could never bully anybody."

"I know. That's her problem." Molly gestured to a pinned-up sketch of a sailboat. "Leo told me: 'I'm using your sailboat sketch on my seed packets,' I go like, 'No way, *fool.*' That's called complicity where I come from."

"Seed packets? What seed packets?"

"You hadn't seen those?" Molly strummed a chord. "Leo got your sister to draw some art for some illegal-type seed packets. You don't think the Alaska police aren't going to see those?" Molly shook her head. "You people live in La-La Land."

Teddy glanced over to the windowsill where dismembered Barbies had been artistically glued back as multi-legged arachnids. "We just might, Molly, but that doesn't mean

Daisy killed her husband. Daisy doesn't think in terms of hurting people.''

"Wasn't much thinking go on with those scissors, now was there?''

Teddy said nothing.

Molly, with utmost concentration, worked her fingers into a complicated bar of all six strings, and strummed. The sound was so piquant and strange, they both waited in silence while it vacated the room. Molly's guitar had a huge soundbox and luscious tone; like the easel, it was blond and new. Finally she said, "Your sister give the coffee back to Michael Havenaw?''

"Havenaw didn't talk to her, he talked to me.''

Molly plucked softly. "He's really something, isn't he?''

Teddy stared, bewildered.

Molly explained: "He has friends in California, grow organic quinoa.''

Teddy tried, desperately, to keep up.

Molly rolled her eyes. "Quinoa's a sacred Inca grain. Agribusiness has kept it from the American people for centuries because they don't want it on the market. The amino acids are practically like meat.''

Teddy lowered herself onto a wooden box. "Molly, I need to ask a favor.''

"I know." Molly nodded. "Otherwise you wouldn't be here.''

"I'm going to Index tonight to bring back the coffee plants and I need to know where the greenhouse is.''

"I can't believe you said that.''

"Molly, we have to get the coffee plants out of there.''

Molly strummed. "I'll tell you what I told Michael Havenaw *and* the police: I don't know anything about the greenhouse.''

"Molly, please.''

"What are you, wearing a microphone or something?''

Teddy stood and opened her coat, then took it off and

turned in a circle. "I have no microphone. I have no interest in getting you in trouble."

"Then you must think I'm awfully stupid."

"No, I don't."

"If I told you I knew where the greenhouse was, that would mean I knew about the other business, which I don't."

"Will you at least give us the keys?"

"Keys?" Molly looked up.

"If you give me Leo's keys, that might give us some idea which locks they go to. Then we could find it ourselves."

"God. You don't get it, do you? You still think I killed Leo." She gestured to the dark sketches on the water-stained walls. "Leo Faber was the first person in my life who wanted me to do my art. Leo Faber bought everything in this room."

Teddy glanced again at the sketches—something was desperately wrong. All the sketches were all right-sided renderings, the left sides smeared in shadows, or not rendered at all. Molly Thistle could only execute lines from the right; she still had enormous amounts of work to do before she mastered her talent. If she ever could.

Teddy leaped up and examined the drawings.

Molly understood, and watched helplessly. She lashed, "Your sister did it. She gets the insurance."

Teddy spun around. "Molly, the police are going to find whoever did it, okay? All we have to do right now is return the coffee plants. After that, nobody will connect you, or any of us, with the greenhouse, or the marijuana, or anything."

"Oh, no you don't. Don't include me, sister. I never had anything to do with any of that." Molly stood the guitar on its heel and hugged it around the middle. "But I might have heard something you want to know: I think I heard that no one's been out to the greenhouse for a couple weeks now, the watering system needs to be reset."

Teddy's eyes swept over the beautiful guitar. "But you're not going to tell me where the greenhouse is?"

"Well, it's been nice talking to you." Molly repositioned

the guitar across her lap. She wouldn't look up.

Teddy grabbed her coat, walked to the door, and let herself out. She drove back across the interstate to the U-district and at the stoplight impulsively bought a clutch of sunflowers from a vendor. Holding the flowers to her nose, she waited for the light.

She pulled up Daisy's steep drive and found herself parked next to the red Oliveri Volvo. On the porch Mrs. Oliveri greeted her with a big smile. "I'm so glad you're home, doll. I didn't think you were going to make it."

"I brought sunflowers for Daisy."

"They're beautiful." Mrs. Oliveri snatched them away. She steered Teddy straight to the stairs. "I've already fed her and she knows you're going out. But you should probably peek in before you leave."

"Leave?"

"Yes, you'll have to hurry. Louie said the dance contest starts at eight o'clock."

11

Alongside Teddy, Sister Bede Kinney sat with hands clasped, the picture of perfect humility and call-to-service. In Bede's eyes danced the question: just how *did* Asian boys in ballgowns fit into the Lord's great Scheme of Things?

Vastly amused, Teddy jotted numbers on her score sheet and watched as Bede tightened her mouth, determined to figure out what it was that set the current contestant, "Miss Lulu Oh," apart from the likes of "Miss Titty-Titty Bang-Bang" and "Miss Coco Lee."

Teddy could tell right away.

Unlike other contestants in the Miss Asia contest, "Lulu Oh" had not borrowed the largest brassiere he could find. A sleek little jock who probably wrestled at 133 pounds, Lulu had had the good sense to put together an upscale posse of Eastside "fag hags" who had trussed him in a tasteful 34B and done his makeup for him. And now, tossing his cheap blond locks, lip-synching the latest Lady Miss Kier, "Lulu Oh" was well on his way to snatching the Coveted Dragon Tiara from last year's winner, All-Conference goalie Derek "Coco" Lee.

Teddy glanced at her pencil lead. If she could no longer convince someone like Molly Thistle that Daisy didn't kill her husband, then it was time to find the killer herself: Kevin

from AgroGene? He was clearly at odds with Dean Havenaw
. . . but, no, they came *together* late Saturday night. Any falling out between them had been since Saturday, and it was
over R-19.

Angus and the white guy, Ghost? But they weren't acting
like killers, stomping around town so big and angry. On the
other hand, both Kevin and Angus *did* know Leo, and Leo
would have certainly let either one into his office. That's it:
she had to figure who had access to Leo's office: either who
Leo would have let in voluntarily, or who could have come
in themselves . . . with *Leo's* key? It was very confusing.

Teddy checked her watch to see what Aurie might be doing. If she could get Aurie to drive to Index immediately after
the contest, they might make the tavern before closing time.
Aurie would also know about the legal "complicity" of designing seed envelopes—Molly Thistle had scared her witless
with that one.

And the guys at the Index Tavern would know where the
town wall was. She and Aurie could load up the coffee plants
and let the marijuana crowd fend for themselves. And there
would be no talk in the car of Daisy's stabbing Leo, because
she hadn't done it, she just hadn't.

Up on stage, Lulu was drop-dead wonderful. Teddy looked
at the scoresheet. If she did award Lulu a "10" in Talent,
Lulu would be tied with Coco for first place, at least on her
tally. She had earlier given Coco a "10"—in Interview—for
saying that he wanted to save the whales by introducing infant
baptism. But Coco had bombed Talent badly, with a mini-
skirted Jimi Hendrix parody so gender-addled it was only em-
barrassing.

Teddy watched openmouthed as Lulu executed an amazing
sequence of dance steps. Lulu stroked the velvet curtain and
sambaed as if she had taken her first baby steps in high heels.
Gyrating stagefront, she slid her hand to her groin à la Michael Jackson, causing animal noises to rise from the audience, male and female alike.

Working to a climax, Lulu raised her hands above her head and waved her feather boa ecstatically. The audience bounded to their feet and lifted their hands too, swaying in the frenzied fellowship of rock and roll.

Offstage Derek Lee stood in the darkness with his arms folded, watching the master at work. A shadow moved and Teddy realized that all the contestants were huddled there, shoeless in their fishnet stockings, astonished at Lulu's polished professionalism.

The music stopped and Lulu blew fevered kisses to the crowd. Even Derek's posse—a petulant pack of Tacoma Mallies—were on their feet for the applause. They mimicked Lulu's hand gestures and analyzed her makeup.

Teddy filled in the rest of her scoresheet and turned it over, waiting for collection. Beside her Sister Bede did the same. Their third judge—a Father Blair, S.J.—had never arrived, having been called to Dublin by family illness.

As they waited, the sound system blared Cindy Lauper's hiccuppy oldie, "Girls Just Want to Have Fun" and the audience swarmed the lobby to empty the vending machines. Sister Bede leaned over knowledgeably. "Wasn't Derek Lee funny with his Jimi Hendrix impersonation?" Bede was showing off.

Teddy handed her ballot to Bede. "Excuse me, Sister, could you turn this in for me? I need to make a phone call."

"Certainly, dear."

Teddy dashed out to the pay phone and punched in Aurie's number. It rang six times and went into automatic message. "This is Aurelien Scholl, I'm not home at the mo—"

"Hello?" It was Aurie, live.

"Aurie! Are you busy?"

"My partners are here. What do you want?"

"You're having a partners' meeting? Now?"

"Wednesday night."

"Aurie, I need someone to go to Index with me tonight, later. I even know who we can ask about the town wall."

He was silent a moment. "Listen, may I call you back? I can't talk right now."

"No, wait, Aurie, I'm not home! I'll call you."

"Fine. I gotta go. Goodbye."

Teddy slipped back into the auditorium to get her coat and tiptoe out. Sister Bede grabbed her arm and teasingly pulled her into the seat. "Now what do you think Father Ricci would have made of all this?"

"Father who?"

"Matteo Ricci, the sixteenth-century Jesuit missionary to China."

"Oh, yes; the man who gave us Confucius. Well, I bet Father Ricci would have thrown up his hands at the whole lot of us and thought we were hopelessly lost souls."

Sister Bede frowned. "You don't mean that. There's a lot of grace here—somewhere." She scanned the room for the lost grace.

"You could hide a bunch in Derek's falsies."

Bede looked away, pretending not to hear.

"May I have your attention, please." At the floor mike was Lisa Murakami, a willowy five-ten cross-country runner, this year's president of the Asian Students Union.

"Ladies and gentlemen, the results have been tallied and we're ready to present awards." Lisa looked toward the doors as the crowd wandered back to their seats. Then she glanced offstage. "As the contestants file out for their final review, I'd like to ask you to give it up one more time for the outstanding job all the guys did tonight."

The room broke into applause as seven graceless, oversized women—plus Lulu—tottered onto the stage.

"Thanks, guys. We love you all." Lisa checked her notes. "Before we announce the top three place winners, the Miss Asia committee has asked me to tell you that the amount raised tonight from the gate and contributions is $718."

Everyone whooped.

"And because we had so many great suggestions about

where to lend our support, the committee voted to divide this year's money among three separate charities. They are: Seattle Domestic Violence . . ."

The audience cheered for Domestic Violence.

"The Old Growth Forest Conservancy."

They cheered on Old Growth.

"And thirdly, the Puget Sound J-Pod of killer whales."

"J-Pod! J-Pod! J-Pod!" chanted the crowd.

Finally the crowd settled down and Lisa looked offstage to cue the next scene. Out from the curtains flitted a short delectable Korean boy rapturous in pink. He was either a bridesmaid or the Tooth Fairy, and carried a satin pillow on which rested the bent—but still sparkling—Coveted Dragon Tiara. The audience *ooohed* with practiced admiration, and the contestants shifted nervously.

"Quiet, please."

The Tooth Fairy curtsied, producing an envelope from his décolleté. Lisa ripped open the envelope and looked up brightly. "Third place, with a total score of forty-eight points goes to Bellarmine Hall's own . . . Miss Titty-Titty Bang-Bang." Titty's posse shrieked with delight while the rest of the audience applauded, still waiting.

"Second place, with a total of fifty-three points, from Campion Hall . . . Derek 'Coco' Lee."

There was a stunned silence, and then the posse of Lulu Oh suddenly realized what had happened. Screams rose like scalded air.

Lisa shouted, "Ladies and gentlemen, this year's Seattle University's own Miss Asia . . ."

Lulu's posse rushed the stage.

". . . Miss Lulu Oh!" Lisa quickly plopped the tiara on Lulu, then dashed out of the way.

Swarming over the footlights, Lulu's posse screamed and cried as if Lulu had just been declared legally dead. Blubbering like babies, they hugged their gal, and then one another, and then took turns trying on the Dragon Tiara. By the time everyone had been hugged and cried over, Lulu's was the only mascara not running down her face.

Playfully, someone pulled off Lulu's blond wig and her feminine allure instantly vanished. He was just a nice-looking Italian boy with ski-jump eyelashes and a red sequinned dress. Someone handed him a soda.

Teddy blinked. Lulu Oh was Louis Oliveri—and Teddy had just voted him the most talented Asian drag queen on campus. "Fusion," she said aloud. Very trendy.

The crowd moved slowly toward the doors, and Sister Bede tugged Teddy's arm. "I'd love to see the boys close up. Shouldn't we go congratulate the winners?" Bede dragged her up the stage steps and they crossed the hardwood. The Lulu Oh contingent fell silent, waiting.

"Louie?

"Hi, Teddy." Louie swilled soda. "Thanks for voting for me. Thank you, Sister."

"Louie, how did you get into the Miss Asia contest?"

He shrugged. "Nobody said we couldn't."

A very Caucasian girl in blue dreadlocks plucked Louie's soda can and took a swig. "We knew he could do it." She dropped her left hand in the limp laid-back fencing posture Louis had affected. "He knew about the hands. Did you see his hands?" She put the soda back in one of them.

"Louie, those are *remarkable* skills. How did you get any studying done?"

"I learned this last year in Rio. The headdresses were too heavy for the women in our Carnival school, so a bunch of us had to dance in drag two days straight."

"I keep forgetting you were at Carnival."

Louie sipped soda. "Yeah, Rio really messes with your head." His face sobered as he suddenly remembered what was going on in Teddy's life and he stepped away from his posse. "My mom says your sister is pretty messed up about Dr. Faber and all. Have they arrested that woman yet?" His eyelashes were ridiculous, but his painted apricot mouth was absolutely luscious. Teddy looked away, murmuring into his ear. "Actually, I was just over to see *that* woman, and I don't think she killed him."

"Yes, she did." Louie nodded strongly. "The same thing happened last year in Rio—the mistress and the wife and all. The police finally traced it to the mistress because she had stabbed him over and over with the wife's scissors. By the time they got to the last episode the whole country was shutting down Monday nights to see who done it."

"Oh." Teddy's face fell. "You mean on TV."

"Yeah, it was the best plot of the year."

"Dr. Morelli? May I see you a moment?" It was Lisa Murakami, and behind her was a simmering brood of fag hags. "Dr. Morelli, we have a problem."

"What is it, Lisa?"

Lisa gestured to the group. "Derek Lee's posse wants to file a protest. They said Louis Oliveri isn't Asian."

Teddy beamed at the girls—one of whom wore a dead rat on her forehead. "You knew that *before* the contest." The rat was certainly rubber.

Wide-eyed, the girls shook their heads. "We never saw him without makeup."

"Yeah, he shouldn't have entered at all. It's like lying or something." Jesuit-trained, God bless 'em.

"Okay." Teddy made a face. "If you really want to file a protest, you'll have to write down all your objections, 1-2-3, make sure you elaborate the reasons for each objection. Make several copies and give one to me, one to Lisa, and"—she gestured to the nun beside her—"one to Sister Bede. Sister and I will come to a decision by—Monday, Sister?—based on how clearly you've argued your case."

"But Derek should take the tiara home. He's at least Asian."

"Just put your objections down on paper, show us all your reasoning."

The girls walked away, still pouting.

Lisa looked at her gratefully. "Thank you so much, Dr. Morelli. And thank you for coming."

"You're very welcome, Lisa." She turned. "Sister Bede, it's been a pleasure."

"Yes, dear. A time of grace. Good night."

Teddy dashed to the upper landing, taking a shortcut to her car. She glanced over to a quiet corner to see, of all people, Renato Silva sitting at a table with a stack of magazines. He saw her at the same time, and smiled.

"Hello," she said. "I didn't know you hung out here."

"Miss Morelli. You're having a pleasant evening?" He tried to conceal the magazines. Which made her curious.

"Do you live close by?" The magazines were Portuguese and stamped "Periodicals Do Not Circulate." *Caminhô*, *Novela*, *Minas Gerais*. How on earth had he gotten them past the sensors at the checkout desk?

Silva squared the pile of *Caminhô*s, an exceedingly gaudy truck magazine featuring a battered pickup in Christmas lights. "We live up the hill. I come here for the quiet." He had no choice but to let her read. She nodded slyly at the magazines. "You must have a lot of pull to take these out."

He smiled sheepishly. "It's a little thing for a homesick man. I bring them back later."

"I'm sure, but you have to tell me how you get them past checkout."

"You mustn't tell anybody, but I roll them in my sleeve and when I walk through the X-ray I am always putting on my hat or my scarf, something high."

She raised her arms skyward to show her size. "If I tried that, I'd probably just aim it at the sensor's best spot."

Silva grinned appreciatively. "Camilla tells me we are needed tomorrow."

"Nine o'clock? And tell her I really appreciate all your help."

"It is a small thing for us. We are happy to do it."

"See you at nine."

"Good night, my dear."

Teddy climbed into the station wagon and drove out Madison Street to Aurie's posh lakefront neighborhood. Under the streetlights, budding plane trees scented the night with raw spring. She braked at the corner of Aurie's cul-de-sac and saw that both his driveway and the entire one-block street were crammed with the Volvos, Lexuses, and sports cars of the eight orthopedic partners.

Twisting the wheel around, she picked her way back to Madison. Even a death was not good reason to interrupt the doctors.

12

Irene Oliveri sat reading in the silent beige living room, minded by a cluster of curious, sweet-tempered bunnies. From the hallway, Teddy drank in the scene, imagining herself just as untroubled and serene.

"Hi, doll. How'd it go?"

"Well." Teddy untied her coat. "You'll be happy to know that your son is the reigning Miss Asia of Seattle University."

"Miss Asia, now what's that?"

"Let's just say Louie's coffee year is paying off in ways you never dreamed of."

Irene closed her book. "Your mother called."

"Marmee?" Teddy spun around. "Where is she?"

"Someplace in Ecuador. Daisy talked to her and I didn't get it all. Daisy was awfully wound up."

"When's she coming home?"

"She didn't say. The weather's bad and she has to take a bus to Quito through the mountains. She'll fly out of there as soon as she can." Mrs. Oliveri stood and her book fell to the floor. Teddy picked it up: *Mary Through the Centuries*, by Jaroslav Pelikan.

"Great book, doll. Have you read it?"

"Don't make me feel guilty. I can barely keep up with Pacific Northwest."

"I want to pass it on to your mother when she gets back. She's the one who said the Church should have deified Mary back in the fourth century instead of deifying three men."

Teddy pressed her lips together. "Third one's a ghost."

"A *boy* ghost or a *girl* ghost?"

"Point conceded."

Mrs. Oliveri walked to the hall and pulled her fox-ruffed parka from the closet. "I miss Maria. Things aren't the same when she's gone."

Teddy pointed to the ceiling. "How'd *she* do this evening?"

"It was hard getting her settled down after your mother called." Mrs. Oliveri tugged on her red kid gloves. "Oh, two things: a woman from the university came by with this," she patted a thick legal-sized document stapled in the upper corner. "She said she was from Dean Havenaw's office and you were supposed to get a copy." Teddy read: AGREEMENT, made this 19th day of January, between UNIVERSITY OF WASHINGTON and AGROGENE-BOSTON.

"Oh, very good." Teddy swept her eyes over the first page, parsing not a word.

"Also, doll, there's something on the machine from when Camilla was here—she won't talk on the phone." Mrs. Oliveri zipped up her coat. "So what's the schedule for tomorrow?"

"Camilla and Renato are coming in the morning, I need to get out and . . . do some research."

"I hope everything's okay, about Daisy needing a lawyer and all?"

"Yes. Fine."

Mrs. Oliveri pressed her cheek to Teddy's. "Well, call me if you need anything. You know where I am."

"Thanks, Mrs. Oliveri. Thanks for everything."

"Good night, doll."

Teddy went back to the kitchen and punched the answering machine. If Daisy was sedated enough, a trip to Index tonight—with Carlo, maybe—might still be possible.

The machine chirped. "Hello? My name is Jeremy Thump." Jeremy had the shyest, weakest voice she'd ever heard. "I'm a student of Dr. Faber's and I need to talk to Teddy Morelli. Anytime tonight is fine." And he gave his number.

Teddy punched it in and waited. A man picked up the phone. "Yeah?"

"I need to speak to Jeremy Thump, please."

"Right. Jeremy ain't here, this is his father. Is this Teddy Morelli?"

"Yes."

"Okay. Jeremy has the professor's coffee trees on our boat at the Old Cannery Marina in Ballard. He said you're supposed to come get them as soon as possible."

"A boat? Is that a fishing boat?"

"Dock two, berth twelve. As soon as possible."

"But how'd they get on a fishing boat?"

"The professor axed Jeremy to move 'em Friday, he said there might be a problem over who owns them."

"But we should call the university immediately."

"No. He s—" A coughing fit stopped him. He hacked vilely into the receiver, as if trying to eject a hairball. This was an ill man. Finally he said, "He said not to give the plants to anybody but Teddy Morelli or the professor's wife. She coming? Or you? Jeremy wants get rid of 'em tonight."

"No, I'll come." Teddy looked out at the gray void of the lake. "But I'm by myself tonight. How about tomorrow morning?"

"Fine. What time should he expect you?"

"Nine, nine-thirty?"

"Nine o'clock. I'll tell him. Boat's the *Mount Holyoke*."

"You're kidding! I have a friend who teaches at Holyoke."

"Yeah, well, good night."

"Thank you. Good night." She slammed down the phone. "*Yeeeee*!" She hopped up and down like a Hollywood Sioux.

But Daisy was sleeping upstairs. Quietly, Teddy darted up the steps, pushed open the door, and tiptoed in.

Daisy bolted upright in bed. "Did you get Leo's keys?"

"Daisy, you're supposed to be asleep."

"I don't want to be asleep."

"What happened to your pill?"

Daisy leaped out of bed and padded to the rocker, groping under the cushion. She was wearing a white flannel gown embroidered with mille fleurs, and looked all of twelve years old. "I can't stand these anymore, they make me woozy." She held out a half-dissolved white tubelet.

"They're supposed to make you woozy."

Daisy dropped the pill on the dresser and plopped back on the bed. "You were just screaming."

"Guess what?" Teddy sunk blissfully into the rocker. "Your brilliant husband moved the R-19 because he thought there might be an ownership dispute. The plants are down at the Ballard docks and I'm going to pick them up tomorrow morning."

"Who called?"

"A student, Jeremy Thump."

"Oh, I thought you were going to tell me a woman." Shivering, Daisy gathered the duvet around her. "Marmee called, she's coming home."

"I know. Mrs. Oliveri told me." Teddy started the rocker with her feet. "Daisy, you know, I think we just might make it through this. I'll run over to Ballard first thing in the morning and pick up the plants. Then all I have to do is make sure we get rid of all the seed packets you designed from the greenhouse. Did you know about that? There's supposed to be this legal thing called complicity."

To escape the tedium, Daisy swooned backward onto the pillows, pulling the duvet over her head. "They only took one box of seed packets to the greenhouse, the rest are down at Bunny Business. Why couldn't you trick Molly Thistle about the keys?"

"Daisy, listen to me. Molly Thistle doesn't have the keys."

The duvet spoke. "Yes, she does." Murmuring, "I just wish I could figure out how she arranged it."

Teddy hesitated. "Yeah, that's a hard one, Daisy. We'll have to think about that." She pumped the chair with her feet and it squeaked agreeably. "But where should I bring the coffee plants? Will they be okay here?"

"I don't know. What does Kevin say?"

"I haven't talked to Kevin—he's the least of my worries. And we still need to change your locks." Teddy rocked the chair. "Molly Thistle gave me a heart attack when she said you could be charged for complicity, but we might be okay on that because nobody could actually prove *you* drew it."

The duvet raised its arm, pointing to the nightstand. "I'm using a seed envelope for a bookmark, if you want to see it."

"Good." Teddy hopped up and teased a colorful seed packet out of Daisy's book. It was a gorgeous four-ink reproduction of Proud Mary, a watercolor that hung in Daisy's office. Above the bunny's head "P-R-O-U-D M-A-R-Y" was spelled out in the whimsical lathwork alphabet Daisy had designed for her Farmhouse Collection.

" 'Proud Mary.' Big deal. How could anybody know it wasn't just some cute little envelope you got printed for your business?" She turned it over: " 'Proud Mary, a compact, low-growing densely branched variety bred for hydroponic applications . . .' So? That could be anything. ' . . . fast germination, high endophyte content . . . specially bred for increased THC content.' What's THC?"

"I don't know."

" 'Quicker to mature than other cannabis—' Oh, dear, even I know that word." Teddy sighed. "Okay, so much for that, we've got to get rid of these." She dropped into the chair again. "So. Nine o'clock tomorrow I pick up the coffee in Ballard, then run down to your shop and get rid of the seed envelopes at Bunny Business. Then all I have to do is run out to Index, find the marijuana, and get rid of those envelopes too. Boy, Angus is going to be mad. I don't care."

The duvet didn't answer; Teddy rocked the chair. "But before I go to Index, I'll drop the coffee off here, but I'd better hurry and read Havenaw's contract. Oh, dear, I need to get myself organized. Or do you think I should call Kevin again?"

A small voice came from the duvet. "Don't go down to the shop tomorrow, the police want it empty, they're going to search it."

"Aaaah!" Teddy sprang from the chair.

"It's okay. I don't have anything to hide."

"The seed packets, Daisy. You designed the seed packets!"

"Teddy, I already told you, I'm finished with all that."

"The cops don't know that. Listen to me: how many packets are at your shop?"

"Four boxes." Daisy plumped the covers.

"Where?"

"In the storeroom someplace—no, wait, Mungo moved them." She disappeared under the duvet. "I don't know."

Teddy ripped the covers back. "Get dressed. We have to go find them."

"No!" Daisy pulled them up.

"Yes. We're going to the shop."

"Give me that! You can go if you want, but I'm staying here."

In one swoop, Teddy ripped the bedclothes off and threw them across the room. "You have to go. I don't know where to look."

Furious, Daisy sat up. She eyed the duvet on the floor. "Teddy, you're so mean. I hate you! You think if you just boss people around they won't notice that you're so *short*!"

In Teddy's little wagon they drove south across the bridge, glancing, as always, at the glittering towers of downtown.

Dreamily Daisy feasted her artist's eyes. "Guess what else Marmee said on the phone?"

"What?"

"The pain of Leo would take seven years to go away."

"Seven? How does she know this stuff? Popee's only been dead five."

Daisy turned. "Don't you see? She makes it up, and it turns out to be true because we believe her."

Teddy gripped the wheel. "That's a pretty good trick."

"I know. That's why, before she left I fooled her. I knew you wanted her opinion about Aurie."

Teddy looked at the jeweled necklace of tail lights disappearing into the downtown tunnels. "Marmee would *never* say anything about our boyfriends."

"That's why I did it."

"What'd she say?"

"I said: 'Poor Teddy, I doubt if Aurie would ever figure out that underneath it all he's suffering from low self-esteem.' And she said, 'He's a fast learner.' "

"She said that?"

"Yes, and then later when I said something about Aurie always manipulating things to go his way, she said, 'But have you noticed how shiny Teddy always looks when she's around him?' "

"I do?"

They entered the downtown tunnels and ocean noises surged around the car. Teddy sighed, "Well, I don't know if much of that is going to matter in the long run. Both of us have been really good at ignoring the fact that ninety miles on weekends is not conducive to a permanent relationship."

"He could relocate to Bellingham."

"Aurie would hate being poor. In his case, it'd be much easier to drop the babe and keep the job."

They popped out of the tunnels and Teddy searched the skyline for her favorite—old-timey Smith Tower. Off the highway at James Street, they rolled down into Pioneer

Square. They waited for a ramble of drunks to cross in front of the car, then pulled into Daisy's parking spot behind the old brick warehouse. Safe in the car, they watched the mirrors until the men had entirely left the area. Teddy climbed out. "Daisy."

"What?"

"Mungo has your key. We can't get in."

"Oh." Daisy slumped back into the car.

"No, Daisy. We have to do this."

"But you just said we can't."

"Who else has a key? How have they been getting in?"

"Reina opens up." Reina was the secretary.

Teddy slid into the driver's seat, key to the ignition. "Where does Reina live?"

"Issaquah."

"Oh, shit."

They stared at the shabby tangerine wall, pebbled with shadows from the high yellow light. Daisy said, "We might be able to climb in the ladies' room. They leave the window ajar."

"Show me."

They clambered out and looked up at the row of frosted chicken-wired windows eight feet above the parking lot. "Which one?"

Daisy pointed to a middle one, the bottom third of which cast a slightly different shadow. "It's open. But there's usually a vase on the sill."

"We need something to climb on." Teddy scanned the lot. "We can roll the Dumpster over."

They trotted over to the green commercial Dumpster. It towered over their heads. It had tiny solid wheels and a steel stairway bolted to the side; it would make horrible noise.

Slithering into the space between the Dumpster and the brick wall, they braced their backs against the Dumpster. Teddy put one foot on the wall. "Okay? Ready, set, push!"

The Dumpster didn't budge.

"Ready, set, push!"

"Teddy, we're not strong enough."

"I know."

They clambered out and Daisy brushed hair out of her face. "What about your car?"

Teddy glanced at her beige wagon, a rich eggy yellow under the lights. "You mean stand on it? The police will notice if it's parked sideways under the windows."

"Back it up, against the wall."

"We can try."

Daisy waited in the shadows as Teddy backed the wagon up under the window, kissing the bumper against the brick wall. She got out and looked. The hatch sloped forward, and they would not be able to make the leap from the roof to the narrow sill.

"Open your hatch," said Daisy. "We'll prop it up and one of us can climb in and open the door for the other one."

"Good, Daisy."

"Aren't you glad I didn't take my pill?" Daisy scanned the parking lot for something to prop open the hatchback. She dashed to the Dumpster and mounted the stairs. "Help me open this."

They banged back the flap and peered at the mess inside. There were forests of flattened cardboard, great basketballs of used mailing tape, bizarro Styrofoam packing shapes. The whole Dumpster smelled of old Starbucks. Daisy sniffed. "Office garbage isn't too bad."

Underneath the Styrofoam was a box of rusty fittings from Uncle Sam's Home Salvage up the street. "Here!"

They rummaged through the box. There were drain traps, angle caps, shutter dogs, steeple hinges, switchplates, slide bolts, and all manner of PVC couplings.

"Just choose something," said Daisy. "We'll wedge it in the hinge."

"It's not like that." Teddy surveyed the pillage. "The hinges are pistons, they whoosh up slowly. What we need is one little thing that pinches the rod so the upper casing can't slide down.''

"Got ya."

They scanned the clutter. "I don't see anything."

"Me neither."

Suddenly Daisy reached in and worked loose a long piece of dense Styrofoam packing. "Let's just prop up the whole rod."

"It won't hold."

Ignoring her, Daisy toted their prize across the parking lot. Teddy followed and unlocked the hatch. The thin black pistons levitated the door until it was high above their heads, the edge stopping six inches from the windowsill—a perfect rampway. Daisy propped the Styrofoam against the lower piston rod, wedging it under the upper casing and into the bottom angle. She saw that the Styrofoam wobbled and would not stay, so she pulled it out and laid it on the gravel. "Give me your keys," she said. She squatted behind the car.

Using the keys, Daisy gutted a trench down the Styrofoam to fit the finger-thick rod. Tiny balls of foam flew off like pearls. When she was satisfied with her work, she reinserted the Styrofoam strut, then reached up with both hands to swing her weight on the hatchback door. The dense Styrofoam compressed a bit, then held. "That should do it. Ready?"

"Me?"

"You did gymnastics."

"You did ballet."

"You're lighter."

Frowning, Teddy scrambled up the car roof, and stepped onto the ramp, waiting. It compressed slightly, but held, and she walked to the edge.

"Just go, Teddy."

She pressed on the panes. Glass shattered inside.

"That was the vase," whispered Daisy. All of a sudden they were whispering.

Teddy pushed in the window as far as it would go and

found it was held by transom chains. It would open only fourteen inches, max. She ducked under the thick iron lip of the upper sash and held on, peeking down at the floor below. Dead jonquils, a broken vase. And this was not going to work: there was simply no way to climb over the hopper window, and jump to the floor below.

"Daisy, I don't th—"

"Climb onto the toilet stall."

Teddy spied the granite walls and twisted her feet around on the narrow sill. Lying flat on the window, she slithered up the panes, her entire weight held by two thin transom chains. She pulled herself onto the top of the stall and looked around. "I'm in."

"Go open the door! Hurry."

"Right." Carefully Teddy climbed down the paper holder, the toilet seat, then hopped to the floor. She dashed down the hall and out across the shop to the foyer. There was a hurried rap on the door. "A bus is coming." Daisy rapped frantically.

"I'm trying. Just a minute."

Teddy swung open the door and they pulled it closed as a city bus rumbled past.

They scampered out into the darkened shop where a thousand questioning bunnies stared down from the shelves. Shafts of street light cast golden patterns on the racks, making the animals look remarkably tanned and well-rested.

Daisy dashed into the storeroom and touched her hand to an empty spot on the shelf. "Gone." She scanned the shelves. "They could be anywhere. Maybe on the shelves in th—"

The floor squeaked, right outside the door. They froze in place, keeping perfectly still. Teddy held her breath, listening.

The floor creaked again and silently Teddy urged Daisy into the cardboard bin of maple blocks used to make Bookshelf Bunny do his balancing act. She wedged herself into a dark corner, her heart thudding bass. Once again the floor creaked.

They held perfectly still.

"Miss Daisy? Is that you?"

"Mungo!"

They climbed from their hiding places as Mungo pushed open the door. Spying his new company, he shoved his hands into his back jeans pockets and broke into a lopsided grin. "Howdy do, Miss Daisy. I'm so glad to see you. I just cleaned up the vase for you."

"Mungo!" Daisy flitted like a fairy godmother. "I thought you were in California."

"Negative." In Mungo's shirt pocket was a fat pack of cigarettes. "I am unable to make that excursion at this time due to financial embarrassment. For recourse I have been living upstairs with a hotplate."

"Mungo, that's terrible! What have you been eating?"

"I hate to admit it, Miss Daisy." He touched his shirt pocket. "But at this point we are down to nondairy creamer and unfiltered cigarettes."

"Mungo!" Daisy dug into her coat pocket and came up with a half-roll of breath mints. Then she unzipped her coin purse and gave him all the folded cash. "I'm so sorry. Please buy yourself something to eat."

"Thank you, Miss Daisy. I will."

"Angus is after you," said Teddy.

"That is correct."

"But you just said you were broke. You don't have his money?"

"Negative." Mungo pulled a flat black wallet from his back pocket and tucked in Daisy's bills. "I know nothing about Angus's alleged finances. And the only person who did was taken from our midst this Saturday night past. Again, Miss Daisy, I would like to express my condolences. I think it was a terrible thing that happened to Leo. Just terrible."

"Thank you, Mungo. That was kind. It's going to take me a while to get used to it, especially since they haven't arrested her yet. But you: you shouldn't have to hide this way. Can't we just explain to Angus you don't have his money? You'd be telling the truth."

"Miss Daisy, I would not say Angus is particularly amenable to the voice of reason right now. My best thought on the matter is for me to lay low until Angus and Ghost take off for Alaska. Herring season opens real soon now, and they got to be up there to pay back on their boat." Mungo shifted his feet. "But I want to know, what are y'all doing here this time of night?"

"Looking for the unused seed envelopes," said Teddy.

"Proud Mary." He nodded, pointing into the shop. "Second material shelf, down in the corner. Saw 'em there last night."

"Oh, good. That was easy."

They ambled out onto the shop floor and Daisy darted into the shelving where the fleeces lay in sumptuous piles.

"*Aaagh*!"

A dark figure suddenly knocked down Daisy and disappeared into the shadows. Petrified, Daisy jumped up and stumbled into Mungo. Mungo stepped back and tripped on Teddy. Daisy scrambled up again and pushed them all into the storeroom. She twisted the deadbolt behind. Panting, wide-eyed, she stood against the door. "My God, Mungo. Who is that?"

Mungo wrapped his skinny arms around his chest. "I don't know. I don't know."

Daisy held up the front of her peacoat, she had ripped off two buttons.

"Daisy, are you all right?"

"I'm fine." Daisy touched the raw threads of her coat. "He . . . he tried not to push me too hard."

Teddy whispered. "His face was covered, or else he's black."

"Ski mask," said Mungo. "High-end polar fleece."

Teddy grimaced. "If it's Angus, why didn't he grab us?"

"That ain't Angus. Angus is about six inches taller than

that. And he never goes anywhere without Ghost.''

"Then who is this?" asked Daisy.

Mungo touched his cigarettes. "Somebody Angus hired."

"He must have followed me through the window."

Daisy nodded. "Whoever he is, he's just as scared as we are. Let's go out and make friends."

No one moved.

Teddy looked up at the high storeroom windows and the sturdy deadbolt on the door. They were safe, but stuck. "I wonder what he wants?"

They waited.

Manfully Mungo twisted the deadbolt and opened the door a crack. "What do you want?" he shouted.

Silence. Noises from the street.

Mungo shouted again. "Listen, tell Angus we don't have his money, and if you just go away, we won't use the gun we have back here."

"Mungo, stop it."

Through the crack they listened for a long time. There was only silence.

"Maybe he's gone," said Daisy.

Mungo yelled through the crack, "Okay, you. We're coming out and we don't want any trouble." He banged open the door. For the ladies. "All clear. We musta scared him off."

Daisy trotted onto the shop floor.

Thwack! A large Peterkins bashed her in the face. "Stop that!" She scooped Peterkins from the floor. "These are too expens—" *Thwack!* Another one hit her on the nose. Defiantly she stamped forward. "I said stop it!"

Thwack, thwack, thwack. A rain of mohair bunnies pelted her in the face. She covered her head, screaming, "Stop it! Stop it!"

Teddy yanked her into the storeroom.

"He's throwing my bunnies!" Daisy sobbed. "Please, somebody, stop him!"

Angrily Mungo stuck his head out the door. "Stop throwing the fucking bunnies!"

"Tell him about the dry cleaning," Daisy sobbed.

"Eighteen dollars every time we send a rabbit to the cleaners. Now cut it out!"

They stood behind the door while Daisy mastered her sobs. Tears ran down her face as she spanked the dirt off Peterkins.

Teddy leaned against the wall. "This is too stupid. If he's not dangerous, why don't we just go out there and tell him we're leaving?"

Mungo grunted. "Let's go." He opened the door. He called, "Okay, you. We don't care who you are, but we're walking out the front door and we don't want any trouble. You can follow us out if you want, but if you so much as lay a finger on the ladies I'm going to get my cutters."

Daisy hugged Peterkins and walked to the door. "I'm ready."

"Let me go first," said Mungo. Cautiously he stepped into the main aisle and looked around. Then he turned, signaling for the ladies to follow. Whoosh! A large Velvet whizzed past his ear. Sasha, Marigold, Kris Kringle in ivory satin, all whizzed by, it was just too much to bear. Teddy grabbed Daisy and an armful of bunnies and rushed back into the storeroom. Daisy was hiccupping, nearly in shock. She hugged her Peterkins and cried.

"Mungo," said Teddy. "We have to stop him." Defiantly she opened the door and shouted. "We just told you, we don't care who you are but you have to stop throwing the bunnies around."

A huge Marigold leaped off the shelf, committing suicide in the aisle.

Teddy giggled in spite of herself. "Sorry, Daisy. Who *is* this guy?"

"That's the problem, he doesn't want us to know." Daisy stroked her Peterkins. "I don't care who he is, just make him go."

"Yes, but how do we get him to leave without losing more bunnies?"

"Persuasion!" Mungo strode over to the cardboard barrel from Vermont and scooped out a maple block. Wrapping his fingers around the hardwood like tentacles, he judged its heft and held it cock-wristed at his side: Piedmont Muni M.V.P., three years in a row. "Ladies, I'm going to have to ask one of you to be bait, if you don't mind."

Teddy stepped forward. "What do I do?"

"I want you to stand in the door and make him angry. Then you gotta duck. Okay?"

"Don't hurt him, Mungo."

"I won't." He opened the door. "Ready?"

Teddy shouted, "Hey, Pigbrain! If you had any sense you'd just run out the front door." Immediately she hit the floor.

Behind her Mungo started a windup. Spotting a moving Kris Kringle ready to be launched, Mungo spun the pitch, hurling the wooden block through the door.

"Aaaah!"

"Got him!"

From the floor, Teddy raised her head. Kris Kringle lay dead at Ski Mask's feet. Ski Mask was clutching his chest in the center aisle, too stunned to move. A second block whizzed over Teddy's head and hit him squarely on the bean.

"Ouch!"

"Sorry, man. Didn't mean to hit you in the head."

Teddy shouted, "Just run out the front door, stupid. It's around to the left."

Ski Mask hesitated, he didn't believe her.

"To the *right*, I mean *your* right!"

Ski Mask dashed to his right, into the shelving and down the aisle to the foyer. They heard the front door bang. They listened. Far away the door clicked shut.

"He's gone." Teddy stood up.

Mungo slipped out into the dark and moments later came back. "Bolt's unlocked. I didn't see him."

Everyone exhaled and walked out onto the floor. "Who *was* that?"

No one had an answer. Teddy turned. "Are you okay, Daisy?"

"No." Daisy scooped up bunnies. "Get a box and we'll take these back to my office." She swatted Sasha across the bottom. "Oh, this is terrible. I don't even want to see these people in daylight."

They worked for several minutes and Teddy finally looked around. "Where's Mungo?"

"Mungo?"

There was no answer. They carried the bunny box to Daisy's office and washed their hands in the ladies' room. When they came out, Mungo was waiting for them, carrying a nylon sports duffel. "Ladies. I'm sorry to leave you, but I feel it is time for me to light out for the orange groves—for real this time. Mr. Ski Mask is no doubt on the phone to Angus, even as we speak."

"Mungo, you can stay at my house if you like. Angus would never bother you there."

"Oh, thank you, Miss Daisy, but I would never put you in that position. The ladies'll be okay here at work, I'm way ahead on the cutting. But if y'all run out, you might let Marlene have a go at it 'til I get back." Mungo cleared his throat. "That is, if . . ."

"Mungo." Somberly Daisy put out a tiny hand. "You will always have a job at Bunny Business."

"Thank you, Miss Daisy. I appreciate that." Awkwardly they shook hands.

Finally Mungo picked up his bag and strode down the hall, boots clomping like the Marlboro Man. "Well, ladies, let's see if I can make it to the bus station in one piece." He pushed the door open with his back. "Y'all take care now, you hear?"

"Thank you, Mungo. Godspeed."

"Well, godspeed to you, too, Miss Daisy."

Mungo disappeared around the corner and they realized they were alone.

"We need to get the seed packets."

"Yes," said Daisy.

They found four printer's boxes on the lower shelf, each bearing a pasted "Proud Mary" packet on the side, a sample of the print job within. They carried two boxes apiece out to the station wagon and hid them in the shadows of the backseat floor. Teddy started the car and looked over to Daisy. "What should we do with them?"

Daisy untangled her seatbelt. "Take them to the pier and throw them in."

Teddy peered down the street to Elliot Bay. She visualized a thick cheery blanket of Proud Marys across to Bainbridge Island. "I know," said Teddy. "I'll ask Aurie if I can use his shredder."

"I thought you said you and he probably weren't . . ."

"No, it's okay. We haven't gotten to that part yet." She put the car in gear and waited for the oil light to go off. "Daisy, how did Mungo know the ski mask was expensive?"

"Because it was. Oh, wait, I know." She crossed her fingers in an X. "It had two seams across the top instead of one. It takes more time to sew."

13

It was time to pick up the coffee.

Mr and Mrs. Silva arrived at eight-thirty in the morning and immediately set up in the kitchen. Renato Silva greeted her merrily, but his eyes were desperately worried. "You will be happy to know I've already returned the magazines. There is no reason to turn me in."

Teddy finally remembered what he was talking about, and smiled. "I wouldn't think of turning you in." Was he having trouble with immigration, or visas?

As the Silvas put away food, she used the extra few minutes to bring the Proud Marys in from the station wagon and hide them under the skirted endtable in the living room. She was in the front hall pulling out her trenchcoat when a gray sedan, a rental, pulled into the driveway. She peered through the glass.

Kevin Hyatt climbed from the passenger side, a two-inch Band-Aid across his forehead. He looked up at the house and dug his fists into the pockets of his Red Sox jacket. From the driver's side, an older man climbed out. He was wearing a camel-hair topcoat and had perfectly groomed short hair—a man from Back East. He glanced sourly at Kevin, and the two of them climbed the steps.

Teddy answered the door before they could ring the bell. "Good morning."

"Miss Morelli?" Kevin stayed back, as if afraid she would hit him.

"Come in."

"Miss Morelli, this is my boss Carter Allsop from AgroGene-Boston, I picked him up last night at the airport."

"How do you do?" AgroGene-Boston extended his hand.

"The airport?" Teddy eyed Kevin's Band-Aid and clucked sympathetically. "Is that where you hurt your head?"

"Yes." Kevin touched his forehead. "A vase fell—in the gift shop."

"Is that right?" She held up her coat. "Listen, I'm sorry to be so rude, but I have an appointment across town in twenty minutes."

Carter Allsop paced a few more steps of the hall, to entrench himself. "We don't mean to take up your time, Ms. Morelli. However, we felt we needed to have a chat before things ran too much farther."

"Please." Teddy lowered her chin. "I'm working on it now. Dean Havenaw came yesterday aftern—"

Allsop jerked convulsively and glanced into the living room. "May we sit down? Just for a minute, please." He tapped a rolled paper tube in his coat pocket. "I have a document I'd like to leave with you—and Mrs. Faber. You need to understand its contents."

She glanced at her watch and led them into the living room. AgroGene-Boston settled on the couch in front of the fleecy mammals who hogged the cushions. Then he stared a full three seconds at Arthur Rabbitstein's tuxedoed backside, probably wondering why Arthur was being punished in the corner.

On the other side of the coffee table, Kevin perched on a blue wing chair. He was wound up like a pin curl.

Allsop pulled out Peterkins and nestled back into the couch.

"Kevin tells me he sincerely believes your family does not possess the R-19 plants."

"Kevin's correct." He must have hung around Bunny Business last night and watched them leave.

"He also says he believes Havenaw and Miss Thistle do not possess the plants either."

A strange way to put it. "No, I'm certain neither does."

Allsop cleared his throat. "Kevin and I also wonder if anyone in your family knows the provenance of the single shrub in Dr. Faber's office the night he was killed."

"That's right." She turned to Kevin. "There was a plant. And you said it wasn't R-19."

Kevin nodded gloomily. "We're having it assayed just in case. But it's not even a university pot."

Allsop proffered the thick legal document. "In any case, Ms. Morelli, even if that single plant turns out to be specimen, it's especially important that you and Mrs. Faber understand the contents of this contract. In addition, I flew out to meet with you in person to let you know that AgroGene means to pursue every measure necessary to assure that R-19 is returned to us safely—all of it, and any productive seed material it may have generated."

Very earnestly, Teddy nodded. "I know. Kevin and Dean Havenaw already told me."

"No," he said flatly. "Not Dean Havenaw."

"Oh?" She kept her face perfectly straight.

"Ms. Morelli, what I'm trying to tell you is that AgroGene—as the sponsoring agency of Dr. Faber's research—owns all rights to R-19. The university owns nothing."

"I see." She leaned against the armrest. "But Dean Havenaw left a contract that says—I assume, since I haven't read it yet—that the university owns the coffee. Now, who am I to believe?"

Allsop curled his lip. "May I see his document?"

Teddy walked out to the hall and brought back the contract. "Yes, here." She flipped to a yellow Post-it. "He's marked this paragraph: 'All rights and title to University Intellectual Property developed under the research agreement belong to the University and are subject to the terms and conditions of this Agreement.' Then he says: 'See definition, page two.' "

She flipped to page two. " 'University Intellectual Property is defined individually and collectively as all inventions, improvements, or discoveries and all works of authorship, excluding articles, dissertations, theses, and books, which are generated solely by one or more employees of the University in performance of the research agreement during the Contract Period.' "

"Oh, dear," said Allsop. "That's unfortunate." He plucked reading glasses from his breast pocket.

"What part?"

"May I?"

She handed it to him.

Peering through his lenses, he skimmed the first page, then turned to the next. "Well, I'm *sure* Dean Havenaw didn't mean to mislead you but, if you read the paragraph following 'Intellectual Property', you will see it defines another kind of research product, *Joint* Intellectual Property. And that says: 'All rights and title to Joint Intellectual Property belong jointly to the University and AgroGene and are subject to the terms and conditions of this agreement.' And"—he flipped pages—"when we go back and see what the 'terms and conditions' of the agreement are, we find paragraph 16, entitled 'Option for a License,' which says:

" 'The University hereby grants to AgroGene the option to elect an exclusive, royalty-bearing license to the Joint Intellectual Property including the right to grant sublicenses.' "

Allsop glanced over his glasses. "And, as you can imagine, AgroGene is fully interested in exercising its option to license here."

Teddy touched his document. "So you're saying R-19 is *joint* intellectual property?"

"That is correct."

She raised an eyebrow. "And Dean Havenaw would say it is only *university* intellectual property?"

Allsop pulled off his reading glasses. "A bit misleading, isn't it?"

She shook her head. "I still don't get it. Why is university intellectual property even defined in the contract if R-19 isn't . . . it?"

"Now, that's a good question." Allsop tucked his chin, scanning the pages.

Suddenly Kevin leaned forward. "I know—sir. The genetic mapping research stays entirely with the university, sir. That needed to be defined in the contract, too."

"Yes, of course." Allsop graced Kevin with a smile as big as a paycheck. Without warning Kevin fell off the chair and landed on his knees against the coffee table. "Excuse me." He climbed back on his chair.

Teddy said kindly, "That's deceptive, that rolled upholstery edge."

Allsop waved the contract, demanding their attention. "At any rate, I hope we've made our point?"

Teddy stood. "You've certainly given me a lot to think about."

The men stood too. "And you understand now that the R-19 is to be returned to AgroGene?"

"I understand that I have a lot of reading to do." She closed her eyes: and she also needed a contract lawyer.

"Yes. Perfectly. I'll leave this copy with you."

"Thank you." She stacked it on top of the identical copy from Havenaw.

"And Mrs. Faber, she'll read it too?"

Teddy looked off into the hallway. "I'm sure, when she's ready."

Carter Allsop smiled genially. "And how is Mrs. Faber?"

"Getting better, I think." She walked to the hall; they followed.

"Good, good," said Allsop. "I'm glad to hear that." He

pulled a business card from his breast pocket. "Please call me if you have any problems with the document. Or have Mrs. Faber call me when she's feeling better."

"Thank you, I will."

"And when the plants become available, you'll call Kevin immediately? He is ready to come get them in an insulated truck, anytime day or night. Right, Kevin?"

"Yes, sir."

"So I'm assuming I can go back to Boston now and everything will work out?" He raised his eyebrows.

"Yes, sir."

The scent of divine sauté began to course through the house. Allsop sniffed. "Smells like a restaurant in here."

She grabbed the doorknob. "Or just good food." It was nine-thirty.

As soon as the men were on the porch, she dashed back to the living room for her coat, then out to the kitchen. Camilla and Renato were at the table trimming limp, out-of-season green beans. Considering the smell from the skillet, the beans would taste sublime anyway. Teddy smiled. "I'm really leaving this time. I have some work down in Ballard, and then out in the mountains, so I'll probably be gone all day."

"Good. Have a good time."

"If Daisy comes down, do you think you could take her for a walk?"

"Oh, yes," said Camilla. "The tulips are coming. It will be quite nice."

Renato smiled in agreement. His dark eyes gleamed. "We hope your search is fruitful today."

She jerked, startled. "What makes you think I'm going on a search?"

Offhandedly, he gestured to her trenchcoat. "You've just tied your coat with the greatest determination. All that is missing is your twenty-league boots."

Teddy smiled and made her goodbyes, driving across the interstate only to snarl herself in Ballard traffic. Delivery trucks hogged whole lanes of Market Street and gum-booted fishermen toted cherished machine parts on their hips like babies.

Down at the docks, traffic thinned out and Teddy crawled Shilshole Avenue looking for the Old Cannery Marina. She found the sign and turned into the gravel lot. A watchman peeked out from behind the curtained window of a huge Alaska storage container. The box was insulated, designed for human habitation, with windows and a door at one end. Out back was play equipment.

Parking the station wagon, she tucked her purse under the seat and pocketed her keys. Her view of the water was entirely blocked by a village of web lockers, numbered and painted blue, like cabanas at the shore. She wove her way through the abandoned city and came out at two gritty work docks, "1" and "2." She trotted down the second.

On either side of the planks weary fishing boats loomed high—purse seiners and gillnetters—their bows nearly touching across the dock. In the oily rainbow corners, dinghies and chase boats hunkered down, full of rainwater, hoping to slack off work.

Teddy picked her way down the scrubby boards. So much oil had spilled over the years that the whole dock looked done up by bootblacks. In a slip near the end was *Mount Holyoke*.

Uncertain, she stopped at the bow. The *Holyoke* was about thirty-five feet long and forty-five years old. It had a scruffy wooden hull painted robin's egg blue—more or less—and a boxy white pilothouse. Oddly, the leading edge of the bow was blunt-nosed and primitive, dropping plumb to the water like a homemade wooden tiller. Protecting the bow was a strange metal strip scabrous with rust. She stared at the primitive bow and chills ran up her spine: the *Holyoke* was designed for breaking ice.

She walked down the catwalk. All along the hull rust bled out like holy stigmata. Midships was the cabin—a pilothouse plus galley—teak-trimmed, well-designed, potentially charming. In the stern the *Holyoke* was completely given over to a massive galvanized spool mounted horizontally to roll net. She stopped a little aft, past the galley. "Hello?" she called.

A man poked his head through the doorway. "Yo?" He was lank and clean-shaven, with clear blue eyes. He wore a navy watchcap to cover his receding hairline, and wearing it, he was almost handsome.

"I'm looking for Jeremy Thump," she said.

"Inside. Come aboard." From the deck he watched attentively, but knew better than to help her. She climbed up the transom and hopped down, landing almost in his chest. "Hi."

"Hi." He had on a clean shirt and a raingear jumper, and smelled of new rubber. He stepped back to let her pass.

She slipped sideways through the cutesy galley door, and squinted in the dim light. Behind her the door slammed shut. She jumped. Out from the bunkroom came Angus. "Hi, there." His black eyes stared like a rabid bull's.

Instantly strong hands groped her from behind, grabbing her armpits. She jabbed her elbows furiously, banging into the stove and door. "Stop it!" she screamed.

"Jesus!" It was Ghost, he was trying to do a pat-down. He held his fingers to his mouth and she raised her forearm across her face, ready to strike or defend.

Angus grabbed her arm. "Calm down. Calm down. We're just checking for weapons."

Ghost stood in the tiny space between the stove and the door, blocking her exit. Up close he was even paler than before. His skin glowed waxy as a church candle and his ghastly white eyelashes made looking at him an act of will.

"Wh-where's Jeremy?" she asked.

"You like that? We made that up ourselves."

Somewhere deep in the hull the starter ground, and ground again. Suddenly the whole cabin shook with noise. Through the small port in the pilothouse door she could see the man in the navy watchcap working the wheel.

"Where are we going?" she demanded.

"For a ride."

"You killed Leo!"

"Oh, shut up."

Suddenly the stack snorted and the boat jerked into reverse. Deep in the hull something alive groaned. Outside, fishing boats began to glide forward. Or, more correctly, she began to glide backward.

"You let me off this boat!"

"Hold still. I ain't finished yet." Bashfully Ghost patted the side pockets of her coat. "You want to lift your slacks for me, or should I feel 'em myself?"

"You touch me and I'll kill you."

Angus cackled delightedly. "Better be careful, Ghost, she might be too much for ya. Want me to get your you-know-what?"

"Stuff it, Angus." Ghost bent over. "Pull up your pants legs or I'll do it myself."

Too numb to resist, Teddy lifted her trouser hems, showing her brown ribbed socks and bare calves. "You can't get away with two murders. Everybody knows where I went."

"One last time, honey: I didn't kill Leo Faber, Leo was my man." Angus blinked sadly. "All I want is what belongs to me. I'm in some deep shit."

"Where are we going?" she asked again.

Angus patted the table to indicate she should sit down with him on the upholstered banquette. She stood rigid by the door. He read her face. "Don't get any ideas, Lamb Chop. The door's locked. Also the door to the pilothouse." Angus patted the table again. "Come on over and sit down."

Ghost prodded her onto the banquette, wedging her in behind the galley table kitty-cornered from Angus. He slipped in beside. "Your name's Teddy." Delicately he lifted her sweater. "Ain't that some kind of underwear?"

She beat him with her fists. "You son of a bitch."

"Stop it! Both of you!" Angus reached over and grabbed her arm. "Ghost, stop it! We ain't gonna do that, you hear

COFFEE TO DIE FOR

me? Lady, he don't mean it about the underwear, he was just teasing. Ghost, tell her you're sorry.''

"I'm sorry." He wasn't sorry at all.

The tall man in the pilothouse peeked through the window to see what the commotion was.

Angus sat down again and indicated she should, too. "We think your name sounds like a cute little stuffed animal, don't we, Ghost?"

"Whatever." Ghost's blue veins were a road map on his skin, his faded hair the color of used bandages. He strode across the galley and opened the hatch to a lower bunkroom. From the hatch he hauled a sea of fishing net. It was silky black nylon with a fine diamond mesh. Outside a parade of masts skimmed by.

"Seen Mungo Henley lately?" Angus tossed his head to throw the black mop off his forehead.

Teddy swallowed. "Mungo's in California." The important thing was to get out on deck before they went through the salt-water locks. She eyed the caulked windows and the slim door to the pilothouse. "You still haven't told me where we're going."

Angus patted her hand kindly. "Alaska, honey. It's just starting to get nice up there."

She jerked her hand away. "I came for the coffee plants."

"We know that. But we have a different problem for you. Our problem is that somebody has to show up at herring season and tell the good folks of Ketchikan and Sitka—"

"—*and* Juneau," added Ghost.

"—and Juneau that their money got lost somewheres down in Seattle, as did the dwarf hybrid seeds we promised. The reason *you're* going to tell them instead of me, is I can only last about two minutes underwater with rocks tied to me."

Meanwhile Ghost hoisted up great pleats of supple netting, gathering them against his forearms.

"Mungo take the seeds?" asked Angus.

Deliberately she took her eyes off the pilothouse door.

"No. And he didn't take your money, either."

"Oh, you can count on that. Well, you tell Mungo, Proud Mary starts showing up in the Central Valley, I'm going down there myself and gut his belly, make him toss his own intestines over the side for fishbait."

Ghost nodded. "I seen that once, stretches back a good thirty feet."

Fear pressed her face, viselike.

"Rabbit Lady got the seeds?" asked Angus.

Teddy huffed, "Her name's not Rabbit Lady." She barely recognized her voice.

"Who's got 'em, then?"

"Th—" She sucked in air. "The seeds are in a greenhouse in Index, Washington. I was going there right after I finished here."

Angus made a face and eased himself out from behind the table. "Yeah? Well, it looks like they screwed us both on that one, didn't they, lady?"

"No, they didn't, I just haven't found it yet. And if you like, I'll get you the seeds when I get the coffee, if you just let me go."

"Lady . . ." He looked down at her pityingly. "There ain't no greenhouse in Index, now is there? We looked, you looked, we looked again. Wore us out, all that looking. Ain't that right, Ghost?"

Like a beneficent spirit, Ghost suddenly showered her with a quarter-acre of black nylon netting, centering it over her head, heaping great piles down her back and onto the table. "Stand up," said Ghost.

She was too startled to move.

"Stand up!"

Covered with net, she eased up out of the banquette. The weight dragged like water. With a fisherman's care, Ghost teased the net onto the seat behind her, then down to the floor.

"Sit down!"

She sat again, and Ghost jerked heaps of nylon from under

her feet and then off the table, tucking it behind the table lip, onto her lap.

"What's this for?"

Ghost ignored her. Working systematically, he slung the loose yardage across the floor, spreading it hand over hand for a full minute, strewing it around the cabin and muddling the edges together. When he was finished he surveyed his work. She sat—helpless behind the table—tucked under a fishnet half the size of a basketball court.

Pushing the hair from her face, she lifted a netted hand. "Please tell me what this is for."

Angus pulled the curtains closed as they approached the locks. "We'll let you out once we get to the straits. But you got to go back under everytime we tie up for fuel."

"Don't she look weird like that? Kinda like one of those black condoms—the quilty kind with Sensa-Probe."

"Shut up, Ghost."

Teddy twisted in her seat. "You can't keep me here."

Angus opened the latch on the tiny refrigerator. It was stocked with Pabst.

She tried again. "I'm going to take off this net and go."

Angus popped a beer. His black eyes blazed crazily although he was calm. "You make us mad when we're going through the locks, we'll show you some of our fancy fishing knots. You going to need a gag?"

Mortified, she clasped her hands together and stared at her stinging knuckles.

"I *said*, you need a gag?"

"No." The tiny nylon knots had already rubbed her skin raw. Tears rolled down her face, unbidden. Deep from in her chest, a wail rose.

"Now you just said you wouldn't do that."

"I'm trying," she sobbed. "I'm scared."

Angus sucked his beer. "Nothing to be scared of. All you got to do in Alaska in talk."

"I—I don't see why I have to go with you." She heaved,

trying to master her tears. "How long will this take?"

"Two, three weeks. And I already just told you. I'm in it up to my ears leasing the frigging *Hollyhock* here and a frigging fish license—I *got* to make payback on herring. But I show up in Alaska without an explanation for my customers, I'm crab bait. So like I said"—he sipped his beer—"you're the one's gonna tell the good folks of Alaska where their money went."

She wailed. "But I was going to Index today, to look for the seeds for you."

"Oh, cut it out. There ain't no greenhouse in Index!"

Ghost's gray eyebrows fell. "Leave her alone, Angus. She's trying to stop crying!"

"Be quiet!" barked Angus. "We're going through the locks."

14

Ghost went out on deck and as Angus baby-sat her—kerchief in hand—Teddy listened to the sound of the Chittendon Locks closing, draining, opening, as Ghost worked lines for the man in the pilothouse.

When they were safely down in the salt water, and Ghost had reappeared, Teddy took a deep breath and peeked through a slit in the curtain. Onshore the flags of Shilshole Yacht Club waved goodbye in the wind.

"I have a question." She turned to Angus. "If I get somebody to bring you money, may I go home?"

"No, it's too late." Angus burped beer.

"How much money?" asked Ghost.

She sniffed and examined their faces. "A thousand dollars?"

"Ha!"

"How much do you need?"

Angus gripped his beer can. "How about *twenty* thousand dollars? You got that much?"

She raised her chin and pushed the hair off her forehead. The black nylon made focus blurry. "I could ask a friend."

"Oh, right."

"That'd be some friend."

"I'm not kidding, I can ask. I just need a phone."

Neither man spoke.

"Get her the phone, Ghost."

Ghost knocked on the pilothouse door and was let in. He came back with a cellular. Laying it on the table netting, he watched while she wiggled her fingers through, pulling up the antenna, unfolding the speaker. She punched in Aurie's office number.

"Seattle Orthopedic," cooed a voice.

"May I speak to Aurie Scholl, please?"

"Doctor's at the training center until afternoon." Seahawks training center. "May I take a message?"

"Yes, please. It's an emergency. Could he call Teddy Morelli at . . ." She held the phone away. "At 386-4636. Thank you." She folded in the receiver, and hugged the phone through the netting.

"No money, huh?"

"He's going to call me back."

They looked away, moved by her innocence. Ghost got up and turned on the tiny TV mounted under the upper bulkhead. "You want something to eat?" He spun around. "Yo, Condom Head, I'm talking to you."

She shook her head.

"I'll take something, Ghost. How about breaking out that acidophilus yogurt?"

"Like hell. That's mine."

"I'll take some yogurt," said Teddy.

"Give the lady some yogurt, Ghost. She's had a hard day."

Ghost handed her grasping fingers a carton of blueberry yogurt and a metal spoon. They both saw immediately that the spoon bowl wouldn't fit through the little diamonds, so Ghost fumbled in a drawer and came up with a tiny plastic spoon. With great difficulty Teddy ate yogurt through the netting, sucking it off the nylon and scraping the bottom of the carton. Ghost ate three cartons and watched TV with special appreciation for the finessed salesmanship of the Necklace Channel.

"Lookit," he snorted between spoonfuls. "They got you thinking they're just *talking* about them earbobs. They're really trying to sell 'em to you."

After two hours the tall pilot came into the galley and Ghost went forward for his turn at the wheel. The pilot opened the refrigerator and popped himself a beer. "Hi." He had gentle smiling eyes. "What's your name again?"

"Teddy."

"I'm Dante."

"His name's Walter," jeered Angus.

Dante ignored him. "You going to be with us all the way up the inland passage?"

"I hope not." She tried to smile.

"I'm sorry about the Jeremy thing. Terrible waste of creativity."

"That was you?"

"Yes." He twisted suddenly. "I brought some books." From a bulkhead he pulled out a cache of paperbacks—Roland Barthes, Miguel de Unamuno, Jose Ortega y Gasset. She smiled gamely and readjusted the net. She had to go to the bathroom.

"They said you teach history?"

She nodded.

"Do you mind if I ask you a question?" Dante squeezed in beside her, sitting on her net. "You know that guy Foucault?"

Teddy blinked. "What about him?"

"Like when he says: 'That's a discursive practice,' does that mean he's anti-Structuralist?"

"Walter, leave her alone." Angus flipped the TV channel to an obese chef carving onions into chrysanthemums and carrots into dahlias. "Been a long time about your phone call, Lamb Chop. Guess your friend ain't going to call back."

"Let me try again." Teddy punched in Aurie's number and was again told he was out.

Dante pulled down *The Order of Things* and waved it in her face. "Is it true Foucault died of AIDS?"

Teddy hugged the phone. "I don't know. I don't keep up with deconstruction anymore."

"Oh." His face fell. "I guess you're a little out of the loop now, your husband just killed . . ."

"My hus—?" She looked at him quizzically. "That was my sister's husband."

The TV chef displayed an adobe hut of cheddar cheese and a saguaro cactus of Monterey Jack. For patio flagstones he had sliced rounds of jicama.

"Oh. I'm so glad," said Dante. "I mean, I'm glad he wasn't your husband. I was going to read you what Unamuno says about grief and co-consciousness, but I guess that's not applicable now."

"No." She twisted in her seat. "I have to go to the bathroom."

"Go ahead, nobody's stopping you," said Angus. "Just don't take off your net."

"But . . ."

"You pee through it, Lamb Chop." Angus read the look on her face. "Hell, rinse it off if you're so fussy."

She slid off the banquette and dragged herself into the tiny toilet off the bunkroom. The door wouldn't close, clogged with net. But she used the marine toilet, looking all the while at the curtained porthole. When she was finished, she pushed back the curtain, and there was Angus's upside-down face, red and smiling. "Boo."

She closed the curtain and traipsed back to the galley. Dante was still at his books, holding open a copy of Unamuno's *The Tragic Sense of Life*. "I have another question." He cuddled close on her net. "Unamuno says that neither faith nor reason can be truly satisfying, but that we have to live *as if* there were a God to make any sense of our lives."

"I haven't read Unamuno," she said.

He was aghast. "But isn't Unamuno like, great?"

Angus suddenly bounded back inside, immensely pleased with himself. They watched as he snatched a potato from the bin and slam it into the microwave.

"Lots of people are great," she said. "But there're so many, we don't have time to read them all. That's why, since Leibnitz, there've been specialists."

"Oh." Dante opened the flyleaf of his book. "Okay, but I need to ask you one more thing. I'm making a list of what people say about belief. See if this is right. With his finger he followed: "Pascal says we have to *wager* there is a God, William James says you're supposed to *will* a God . . ."

Frustrated, she pulled at the net.

". . . Kierkegaard says you have to make a leap of faith, and our buddy Unamuno says we must 'live as if God exists.' " He paused.

"Sounds good to me."

Dante leaned close. "That's not what I mean. I want to know, which one is right?"

"Dante, I don't know what to tell you. What they're all saying has been a very common idea ever since the Age of Reason—acting *as if* there's a God. That seems to be everybody's best idea on how to keep moral order."

"But Unamuno's a little better, right? I mean, besides his leap of faith, he says here, quite beautifully, I might add, that ' . . . the common bond of brotherhood and compassion in the world is the deepest satis—' "

"Walter, shut up!" Angus threw a copy of *Bait* magazine.

Dante closed his eyes in contempt. "Angus, we were having a philosophical discussion here."

"I heard your discussion, dickhead. And there *is* no fucking brotherhood of compassion in the world, otherwise I'd still have my fucking twenty thousand dollars."

"It's a matter of judgment, Angus—knowing the difference between invertebrates like yourself and authentic human beings." Dante clutched his book. "Your problem is you couldn't tell an authentic human being from the fish gurry in the bottom of the boat.''

"Wrong, dickhead. My problem is, I give an authentic human being like Leo Faber a wad of cash big as that potato—and that's okay because he's a class guy and I can trust him. But then some other dickhead comes along and whacks off my class guy, runs off with my cash. So it don't matter shit about brotherhood and compassion, dickhead, because somebody else is always playing by the dickhead rules.''

Teddy gaped at the roly-poly Idaho circling the bottom of the microwave. "No!''

The men stared.

She shook her head. "My sister has that money.'' With thumbs and fingers she made a potato-sized 0. "Does it have a hundred-dollar bill on the outside and a blue rubber band?''

"My money!'' Angus popped out of his seat. "Where is it?''

"Daisy has it, at least she did.''

Angus paced the floor. "Well, call her on the phone. Jeez, let me tell Ghost. Ghost!'' He dashed into the pilothouse.

Through the netting Teddy once again pulled up the antenna, this time punching in Daisy's number. Ghost crashed into the cabin and the three men hovered like June flies.

Daisy's phone rang, and rang, then the answering machine clicked on. "Camilla?'' Teddy said. "Daisy? Please pick up the phone.''

Through the open door, Ghost steered with his foot. "Rabbit Lady ain't home.''

"No, she's home. It's just that the woman helping her doesn't like to talk on the phone.''

"Trouble with the police?''

"She has an accent.''

Sagely Dante tented his fingertips. "Accents are often so beautiful you hear your own voice sing in new ways.''

"I'll try again.'' Teddy punched in numbers and again the

answering machine clicked on. "Camilla? Daisy? This is Teddy. Please—"

" 'Allo?" It was Camilla.

"Hello, this is Daisy's sister. May I speak to her, please?"

"Certainly. One moment, please."

She waited while the men flitted around the table.

"Teddy?" Daisy sounded eight years old.

"Daisy, listen to me. I'm on Angus's boat and we think the money in your underwear drawer is his."

"Oh, good. When are you coming home?"

"That's the problem. We're out on the water and they won't let me go without the money."

"You mean—" She fumbled with the phone. "Just a minute, let me go upstairs."

In a few seconds Daisy was back on and the phone clicked downstairs. "You mean they've kidnapped you?"

"Yeah, I guess."

"Teddy, are you okay?"

"I guess."

"Where do I bring the money?"

"Ballard. Just a minute." Teddy put a hand over the receiver. "She can bring the money. How long will it take us to get back?

"*Unlikely.*" Angus checked the shoreline. "Tell her to hike it on up to La Conner. We can meet her at the La Conner Pier in an hour and a half."

"Did you hear that, Daisy?"

"La Conner Pier. But what about Camilla? Renato's not here now . . ."

"Daisy. Please—"

Angus shouted, "La Conner Pier, hour and a half."

"I heard him," said Daisy. "I'll be there."

"Look for an old blue boat," said Teddy. "The *Mount Holyoke.*"

"Holyoke? Isn't that where Barbara teaches?"

Teddy could barely answer. "It's not the same." She folded the phone.

The mood was instantly festive and Angus slid a CD into the player. To the throbbing of the Grateful Dead they motored up the beautiful inlet, snow-capped mountains circling the edge of the world. Far ahead the Canadian range gleamed silver-white, like steel on a retro diner.

Teddy pulled herself up and padded into the pilothouse to chart their progress. She rubbed her forehead furiously and gritted her teeth. "May I take this thing off now? It's really frustrating."

"Suck it up." Ghost steered with his finger.

She went back to the galley and flopped down, trying to let Jerry Garcia tease her into a better mood. Thumbing *Bait* magazine, she noted quickly she would never need its advertisers. She read it anyway and was deep in an article on gutting sea urchins when Ghost called out, "Pier's to the right?"

She leaped up and looked out. They were chugging up the Swinomish Channel with an antique red cannery off starboard and a retirement village to port. High over their heads was the La Conner Bridge—startling orange geometry suspended over the slough. Angus nudged her shoulders. "You go back in the galley and sit down." He turned. "Walter, if she fools around, dump her in the bunkroom."

"Yo, my cap-i-tan."

"Fuck it, Walter."

They tied up with a gaggle of motorboats in front of a freshly painted ivory building signed *La Conner Pier*. Noting the age of the adjoining boaters, Dante turned off the music. Daisy's yellow Mercedes wasn't in the parking lot, nor was a person resembling Daisy.

Teddy peered from the window. "She probably got caught in traffic."

Dante's blue eyes gleaned. "It's no matter, really. If she doesn't come, we can make you quite comfortable here. There's so much to talk about on our way north."

Angus and Ghost wandered in and out the cabin fussing with the gear, the boat, the charts. They waited. After an hour the silence became unbearable. Ghost finally cleared his throat. "Angus, you wanted to do Anacortes by nightfall."

Angus looked out the window. A blush of pink bloomed at the edge of the sky. "I know. I know."

"How much longer you want to wait?"

Angus eyed Teddy. "Call Rabbit Lady again."

Teddy punched the numbers. "She won't be home." As expected, the machine picked up the message. "No."

Angus stood. "Well, that's too bad, I almost thought we were off the hook. Ghost, Walter, we need to get moving."

"Please," she begged. "Can't you wait a little longer? Traffic's heavy through Everett."

Dante pulled off his watchcap, vulnerable. "But if you stay, we can buy books in Anacortes, there's an excellent shop on Commercial . . ."

Out from town rolled a large maroon sedan, newly familiar. "Wait a minute!" yelled Teddy. She couldn't remember whose car it was. The sedan pulled in next to the fishing pickups and Daisy leaped from the back seat.

"It's my sister!"

"Shut up, there's guys on the next boat."

Teddy bit her lip and watched from the galley window. Daisy strode boldly to the dock carrying a oversized woven handbag under her arm.

"Daisy," she breathed.

From the driver's side of the sedan Mr. Silva climbed out and stood attentively by the car. In the front seat a moving white shape was Camilla. Teddy clawed at the net. "Can I take this off now?"

"Go ahead. But don't go outside. We wanna make sure she's got the money first."

Dante and Ghost quickly found the selvage of the net and helped her clamber out. She breathed deeply and relaxed, calm in a way she didn't realize had been missing.

They watched Daisy tread down the dock. Ghost murmured, "Angus, we work this right, Rabbit Lady'll give you all the money in her purse."

"Hmm."

"The spic looks like he might be big bucks, too . . ."

"Don't do that!" Teddy pulled Angus's sleeve.

"Shut up."

Teddy shoved her knuckle in her mouth and bit down hard. Angus pressed her on the back. "Go outside and stand on the deck, right next to the door. And don't open your mouth, get it? Otherwise we'll drag you back down the hole."

Teddy nodded and scrambled outside. The wind was achingly sweet. She stood beside the galley door as Angus held onto the back belt of her trenchcoat. "I'm right here, Lamb Chop. Don't try anything." When Daisy was within eye-contact, Teddy darted her eyes right, and left, and made a worried mouth.

Daisy watched the funny face, confused. She walked forward. Frantically Teddy contorted her cheeks and rolled her eyes back and forth.

Without interrupting her pace, Daisy dipped her hand deep in her purse, flashed a green roll of bills and walked deliberately past the boat, right to the end of the dock. All around her, yachties swarmed over their tied-up crafts.

"Where's she going?" barked Ghost.

At the far end of the dock Daisy turned and waited. She shifted her purse under her arm.

"What's she doing?"

The men stared.

"Wa-hoo!" Angus yelped in admiration. "Rabbit Lady's dropping a con. Look at her, Ghost! She beat us at our game."

All around Daisy were busy dock folks, certain to take interest in any shouted ransom exchange. Angus had no choice but to play her way. "God, she's got balls!"

On the end of the dock Daisy glanced up at the bridge, the sky, the artfully painted sign. She waited.

"What are we going to do?"

Angus grinned. "We're cool. All she wants is her sister." Angus nudged Teddy in the back, still clutching her trenchcoat. "Hop up on the transom."

Teddy scrambled up on the thick side and Angus stood behind, holding her by the belt.

Satisfied, Daisy turned and started back down the dock. As she walked, she plunged her hand deep into the bag. Her face was a hardened mask.

The men watched. Deep behind Daisy's eyes sudden malice burned. Teddy stared; something awful was going to happen. Daisy's hand went deep into her purse.

"She's got a gun!" yelled Ghost.

Daisy strode, relentless.

Instantly all three men hit the deck.

Then Daisy was upon them. Flinging the money into the boat, she grabbed Teddy by the hand. "Hurry, hurry, hurry," she panted. She jerked Teddy forward. "Don't look back. Just keep walking." Stiff-legged, they hustled away, trying not to run. "They can't get us. Mr. Silva's watching."

"I'm fine. I'm fine," huffed Teddy.

They scrambled along the asphalt shore path. Behind them a boat engine fired.

Mr. Silva waited at the edge of the parking lot. Reading their frantic faces, he opened his arms to them. "My darlings!" They leaped into his embrace. "My darlings, is everything okay?"

Unabashed, they hugged the poor surprised man. "Something is terribly the matter," he said. "We'll call the police?"

"No, no. Everything's fine, Mr. Silva. Thank you so much."

"Are you sure, my darling? They have taken nothing," he hesitated, "of value?"

Teddy thought of the big new Ben Franklin, his mouth

gagged by a blue rubber band. "No, nothing of value at all."
She turned to watch the boat pull away, Dante holding fast
at midships. He snapped her a jaunty salute.

Mr. Silva bustled them into the back seat of the sedan and
started the engine. Camilla turned, surveying their faces for
information. At Renato, she unleashed a blitz of Portuguese,
continuing to prod him until she was satisfied. In the rearview
mirror, Mr. Silva said, "Camilla thinks we should go to the
police."

Teddy sat forward. "I doubt we would have anything to
tell them. All we were doing was returning some money to
those fishermen. They have to go to Alaska."

The Silvas still looked doubtful.

They sped silently down Interstate 5, Teddy grateful that
rush hour traffic was going the other way. As they entered
North Seattle she glanced at her watch—six o'clock. "I need
to be dropped off in Ballard, my car's there."

They left the highway, and took a full thirty minutes to
push down into Ballard. They pulled into the Old Cannery
Marina just at dusk and Teddy whispered to Daisy. "I still
have time to get out to Index before night."

"Teddy, no!"

"It's okay. I'm going to ask somebody to come with me
this time. I'll be fine."

Daisy looked away.

They drove past the looming storage container, now vacant,
and through the little village of web blockers. Across the
empty gravel lot, something was terribly wrong with her car.

"Oh, no!"

The station wagon was propped on cinder blocks, ob-
scenely displaying its naked axles. Teddy hopped out. In addition, the front headrests were gone, the passenger window
smashed in. She ran up: not just the headrests: both bucket
seats had been stripped from the car. The tape player was
missing. She opened the unlocked driver's door—her purse,
of course, was gone, too.

Mr. Silva walked to the front of the car. "Open the hood, my dear."

She pulled the inside lever and Mr. Silva raised the hood. They peered in. A airy gaping hole was in the place of her battery. "This is a mess," he declared.

Camilla and Daisy came around front. "Teddy, your license plates are gone."

Mr. Silva slammed down the hood. "I must insist, now is time to call the police."

15

Next morning the phone rang at eight. "Hello?"

"Teddy, I'm outside on the porch. Would you please answer the door?"

"Aurie!" She jumped out of bed and ran downstairs. Through the etched glass he was still folding his phone. He waited while she unlocked, smiling down at her plaid flannel.

She inhaled his leather jacket. "This is a surprise."

"I thought you wanted see me?" Along with his phone he carried a road map. He leaned over and kissed her head.

"Oh, Thursday." His day off. She found Daisy's Cowichan Indian sweater in the closet and zipped it on. It weighed at least five pounds.

He watched, then loped Aurie-like back to the kitchen. "That was a very strange phone number you left yesterday—what was that all about?"

"It's okay. Everything worked out."

"Good." Aurie sat at the table and unfolded his map. "So what is Dante's Poetry Service? And where's your car?"

She bit her lip. "My car's in the shop." She put on hot water for coffee.

"He offered to make me a couplet."

"Who?"

162

"Dante. He also said not to let you go to Index alone. Is . . . is this something I should know about?"

"No." She shook her head. "Not at all."

"Well, I agree with him." He nodded to the driveway. "I hooked the yard trailer on the car, we can carry the coffee plants under tarps."

"Aurie! Thank you." She rushed over. "My purse got stolen yesterday so I was going to drive without a license."

"We're just one catastrophe after another, aren't we?" He searched her face.

In the freezer she plied through Daisy's cache of coffee beans—decaf, black espresso, Irish Cream.

Aurie said, "You still don't seem happy to see me."

"Nonsense. I'm very happy."

There was a noise out front and Mrs. Oliveri appeared on the porch toting a girl-type cherub. Teddy rushed to the front door. "Good morning!"

"Hi, doll. You know my Amy, don't you?"

Teddy jiggled the cherub's hand. "Hi, Amy."

Self-conscious with the attention, Amy pulled up her shirt to show a thick surgical adhesive spotted with purple Barneys.

"Oh," gushed Teddy. "I love Barney!"

Mrs. Oliveri shifted her granddaughter to the other hip. "Amy just had a tummy operation, and now she's all better. Isn't that right?"

Amy nodded, agreeing to this lie.

"How's Daisy today?"

Teddy led them back to the kitchen. "I don't know yet. I think she'll sleep pretty late. We had a rough day yesterday."

"I'm sorry to hear that. No word yet from Maria?"

"I'm afraid to call Carlo again. He's pretty snappy."

Bathed in soft light from the lake, Aurie stood by the window, waiting.

"Mrs. Oliveri, this is Aurie Scholl. Aurie, Irene Oliveri."

Aurie nodded. "We met Sunday."

"And Dr. Scholl, my husband reminded me that it was one

of your partners who did our son's knee last summer.''

"Ted Molaski. Remembers Louie very well, says he's a great kid.''

"Thank you.'' Mrs. Oliveri bussed Amy on the cheek. "We like him.'' She plopped Amy on a chair and peeled a banana from her purse. "Are you taking Teddy someplace?'' She gestured to the map.

"Index, Washington,'' Aurie sat down, "which is off State Highway 2, which is north of Everett. Looks like it'll take about an hour and a half.''

Mrs. Oliveri swiftly broke the banana in little bits and put it on a plate. "Good. Teddy needs to get out, she's been cooped up here all week.'' The hot water began to rumble on the stove. "Doll, why don't you get dressed? I'll make the coffee and keep Dr. Scholl entertained with Amy's surgery.'' She glanced at Aurie's face. "I'm kidding, I'm kidding. Go get dressed, doll. I'll take care of this.''

Ten minutes later Mrs. Oliveri shooed them out the door, handing Teddy half a bagel and a covered cup of coffee. Teddy stuffed her borrowed makeup bag—packed with Kleenex, Chapstick, and key fob—under the seat, and they drove the highway north into the blue morning. The bagel, she gobbled in four bites.

Aurie whistled gamely through his teeth and checked his garden trailer in the rearview mirror. "I think we might get Cosmic Mountains this morning.''

She swallowed coffee. "What are Cosmic Mountains?''

"That's when you get Mount Baker in the windshield and Mount Rainier in the rearview mirror.'' Aurie fine-tuned his mirrors. "If the weather's good you get Cosmic Mountains for about five minutes through Everett.''

She checked her mirror, too, and noted the position of Rainier behind them—a dense white pyramid entirely out of context with its surroundings. "I didn't get enough breakfast.''

"Tell me when you want to stop.'' He glanced over, eyes dancing behind his horn-rims. "Speaking of no breakfast, the insurance company ran us all through hematology last week. And guess what?''

"What? No, wait, you're telling me this so I'll know your blood's clean."

"Yes, indeed. In fact, my blood's so clean the leukocytes have formed a book group.''

She smiled and looked out the window. "That's cute, Aurie."

He tried again. "Then I guess you haven't noticed my new strategy."

"What strategy?"

"I'm playing hard to get."

She squelched a smile. "Fine, Aurie. You keep playing."

"Yes. But what you don't seem to realize what you're missing out on. I'm the best lay on the whole fourth floor. You should *hear* those guys talk."

She looked away. "Laying is done in pairs, Aurie."

"Vixen!"

"Aurie, listen. If you could explain to me how we run a long-term relationship from three counties apart, I would love to entertain the thought of getting serious with you."

"Ha!" Aurie grabbed high on the wheel. "Dick Yancey *told* me that!"

"Told you what?"

He grinned broadly. "He said in med school he figured out that to get women to go to bed with you, all you needed was a few prepared sentences about *why* it should happen. Once you said that, they'd go down like felled trees." Aurie glanced over quickly. "If you'll pardon the analogy. He says he doesn't understand it either."

"What's not to understand? All we're asking for is a reason to go to bed."

He turned quickly, "Why do you need a 'why'?"

"Why *don't* you need a 'why'?"

He checked his trailer in the rearview. "This is one of those inscrutable things, isn't it?"

Teddy sighed. "I think so."

He looked over sharply. "You using any birth control?"

"I refuse to answer that, Aurie."

Brooding, he drove north through Everett where both mountains had long since disappeared behind navy shrouds. He turned east towards the foothills, driving into darkening weather. By the time they got to the fairgrounds in Monroe the blue air had turned mizzly and Aurie switched on the wipers. They rode in silence past the towns of Sultan and Startup, and Aurie slowed down at Gold Bar. "These burgs are getting progressively smaller. Do you want to stop for breakfast?"

Drops plashed the windshield, she shook her head. "I'll pick up something at the Index Tavern when we ask for directions."

"Pickled eggs?"

"Beef jerky . . ."

And then came the sign: *Index, 1 Mile.* They turned onto the dark canyon road.

The storybook river babbled past on their left and Aurie tried not to crash the car as he craned to look at the black granite canyon. "Humidity's different here. I bet this has its own microclimate."

"Stop!"

Aurie braked.

"Turn here." She pointed to the one-lane bridge.

"You've got to be kidding." Cautiously he turned onto the wooden bridge. "How's our trailer?"

"Fine."

At the other end of the iron trusses the Twinkie truck waited for them to pass. High above, limp clouds hung like laundry on the cliff. Near-rain gathered on the windshield, ready to pool in droplets.

"Tavern's on the left," she said.

He veered into its lot. "Closed."

She hopped out and read the fine print. "It doesn't open

until ten. Who can we ask about the town wall?''

"The place is small enough, let's look ourselves.''

"I already did that, Aurie.''

"Will your feelings be hurt if I'm a better looker?'' He guided the trailer down the main street, peeking—as she had—into front yards on the river.

At the end of the street, he turned. "Why didn't you say it wasn't on the river?''

Crossly she twisted in her seat. "Is this what married people do?''

"No.'' He turned another left. "Married people are not allowed to venture more than ten miles from the interstate in case one of them suddenly needs a mall.''

"Hush, Aurie.''

He drove back the two blocks of town. At the far end was a clapboard roadhouse with a rose garden out back. "Bush House,'' he read, "1898.''

"I'm hungry.'' The white clapboards were genteel and welcoming in a way a tavern could never be. She thought of teapots and cloth napkins, and eggs with perfect yolks. "The cars out front are a good sign.''

"Sedans,'' he murmured. He pulled onto the gravel at the side.

They walked into the long dining room with its forest green wainscoting and Windsor chairs. Sepia pictures of Index-Past showed men slicing walls off the canyon and felling huge trees. They sat at a table by the window and listened to three men in plaid shirts critique the performance of the Startup Volunteer Fire Department—not quite as good as the Index VFD, it seemed.

Aurie murmured, "Would you still love me if I were a fireman?''

"That's a trick question, isn't it?'' She opened the menu and rejoiced in the offerings: eggs Benedict, omelets, waffles, fruits in season, bounty of all kinds. The waitress came.

"I'll have a Denver omelet and a pot of tea. Whole wheat toast, please." Teddy handed her menu back.

"Blueberry muffin and coffee."

They ate in silence, watching the late breakfast customers finish their coffee and leave, table by table. By the time Teddy had finished her omelet they were the only people left in the room. The waitress came out with the coffee pot and refilled Aurie's. As she poured, the ceiling squeaked alarmingly, as if a tractor-trailer had rolled across. They looked up and the waitress said, "Oh, don't worry about that, it's just our ghost."

"Where'd you get him?" Teddy sipped her tea.

"Her. She was a mail-order bride from Iowa, hung herself upstairs by mistake."

Aurie set down his cup. "You do know you have to tell us the whole story now?"

"Of course." The waitress grinned. "Her name is Annabelle and she came out in the early 1900s to marry a miner who had written Back East for a wife. So Annabelle putts on out here, hops off the train, and finds out the fiancé had stood her up, he wasn't there. Worse than that, Annabelle was down to her last fifty cents. She checked in upstairs, stayed a couple of nights, then somebody asked her about her bill. So that night she hung herself.

"Next morning the fiancé shows up—he'd just then dug himself out of the snow up in the hills—and when folks told him about Annabelle, just about broke his heart. Just about broke the whole town's heart."

Teddy nodded somberly. "That would."

The waitress looked out at the mist and low clouds. "Think it still hangs over us."

"And it's the kind of story that'll always get passed on." Teddy gestured to the rainy green lawns and hothouse shrubbery. "But something else is operating too, I think. Index seems like a *blessed* place in some way—and not just because it's lost in a time warp. Do you know why that is?"

The waitress's baffled face said she had no idea what Teddy was talking about.

Teddy swallowed tea. "I guess if you actually live here, you don't notice it."

Aurie said, "I know what you're talking about, I was telling you when we came in. This is one of those little mountain pockets with its own microclimate."

Eagerly the waitress nodded. "That's right. You should be here on an August afternoon. Heat coming off the Town Wall is so strong it keeps the whole place warm 'til next morning."

Teddy clattered down her teacup. "The Town Wall is the cliff back there?"

"It's 2,200 feet straight up. Rock climbers love it."

"And if we wanted to go *behind* the Town Wall we just follow the road south around the bluff?"

Her face clouded. "Yeah, I guess. But there're an awful lot of old logging roads back there—fire roads now. I'd be careful about getting lost."

"So none of it is on a map?"

"Are you kidding?" The waitress cleared their plates. "I get excited when I find *Index* on a map."

They paid the bill and went outside, inhaling the wet mist. It was nothing like city air, it was so heavy with water and oxygen that a deep breath actually cleared the vision. They climbed in the car and she said, "Mungo told me 'right behind the Town Wall.' Should we just go wander around?"

"I guess." Aurie turned on the wipers and drove a block to the riverfront street. Suddenly at the bridge he turned left.

"Where are you going?"

He rolled to a stop in the gravel beside the volunteer fire department and climbed out.

"Good idea." She joined him.

They tried the front door—the small one for humans—and found it locked. Tramping around back, they tried another door, and walked right in. The airy garage held a boxy red Hahn engine and a spiffy new medic van. Between the two vehicles was a trailered blue rescue river raft—latest local attempt at keeping one step ahead of the Seattle tourists. Teddy and Aurie walked into the office.

On the wall was a sweeping map of the local fire district. Each empty forested square mile was gridded and numbered. At the far east corner of the map, the puny area inhabited by humans was paved with blue scribble.

Aurie squinted at the map. "Look. To go around the cliff, we go back to the Bush House and take that road out of town."

The Bush House road wound around a bit and ended in a maze of dotted lines. "Those must be gravel," said Teddy. With her finger she followed the dots. "Aurie, *behind* the Town Wall could mean any of these."

"Yes, but I'm assuming the greenhouse is wired?"

"Sure. Growlights."

He pointed. "Then we only need to try lowland roads. Roads with switchbacks up into the hills aren't going to be carrying power."

"Good point, Aurie." She stood on tiptoe and peered at the dotted road he liked. "Forest Road 7099."

"What do you think?" he said.

"Let's go."

Outside the air had settled into a soothing all-day mist. They climbed in the car again and drove past the Bush House. The wet pavement glowed pearly gray and Aurie's fat wipers cut bright wedges of clarity. After a few blocks of "suburban" Index, they found themselves in a maple bog, the road persisting right, hugging the south face of the cliff.

A mile outside of town they came to the scarred granite flank of the old quarry and Teddy scanned the open site: nothing remotely resembling a Quonset hut.

They crossed railroad tracks and the road disintegrated into gray gravel. A bit farther on Aurie braked suddenly at a Y in the road. "This wasn't on the map."

"Should we go back and check?"

"Naw." He muscled the wheel. "We're not lost yet."

They followed the gravel road into a series of unmarked intersections, always electing a right turn. "I haven't seen power lines in a long time," said Aurie.

"Me neither."

They listened to pinging gravel on the Saab and looked out at fat maple trunks carpeted in bright green moss. Nestled in the mosses were ferns, hanging from the ferns were lichens. The undergrowth of salal was high enough to hide a deer.

After several turns Teddy looked up and saw they were genuinely on the back side of the Town Wall. Past it, even. There was no greenhouse ahead. "Aurie, it must have been one of those dirt tracks back there."

"There weren't any power lines," he muttered.

"There're none here either."

They drove slowly, looking at both sides. At a wide spot ahead a polished steel chain linked two concrete stanchions blocking entry to an earthen two-track. Aurie stopped to turn around.

High above, the towering backside of the cliff loomed like Godzilla. Teddy glanced at the chain: it was steely and high-tech—very mean-looking—like something she had seen recently. "Aurie, stop."

She hopped out and crunched across the pale gravel, squatting in front of the stanchion to peek into a four-sided lockbox. Inside the metal box was a serious steel padlock with an outsized shackle. She turned it over. "Amloy!"

She ran back to the car and grabbed the makeup bag. "Aurie. This is it, Amloy."

"Amloy?"

Fumbling with her keys, she ran back and slipped the slim blade into the keyway. It turned like a knife in soft butter. The chain fell heavily onto the ground, and she picked it up and dragged it off the track. She climbed back in the car.

"What about power lines?" he asked.

"Aurie, this is it."

They wove through the gray maple trunks, making their way toward the cliff. Finally, through the trees they spied the Quonset hut crouching at the base of the near-vertical slope. It was thirty feet long and painted the pale chalk green of old hospital hallways. On top, its ribbed corrugations grew such a crop of black mold that the whole humped building looked like a giant sea-striped crustacean. Sprouting from the unseen back wall were blower stacks, like prehensile antennae.

Aurie circled the car around, positioning the yard trailer by the door. "I hope it's the same key."

"Got to be, he only mentioned one."

They climbed out and padded across the rich humus. Black mud squished up with each step.

"Listen," said Aurie. Off to the right was a chugging shed the size of an extra-large doghouse. Out on the gravel road was the sound of a heavy car.

"To what?"

He pointed to the shed. "Generator. That's why there're no power lines." Mounted beside the generator shed was a fifty-five gallon fuel barrel.

"I wonder where they get their water." She looked around.

"Probably a creek."

They mounted the stoop, a simple construction of firewood laid perpendicular to the door—now half-sunk in the mud. The door was overlaid with metal sheeting and fitted with a chunky doorplate around the lock. On the lockface, the friendly word: "Amloy."

Aurie perched himself on the firewood stoop and held Teddy's elbow to help her keep balance. An engine noise in the woods made them look up and they saw dark movement through the trees. It was a van coming down the two-track. They squinted at the windshield but could not see the driver.

The black van pulled up and stopped. They waited. Strangely, Renato Silva climbed out. He was wearing a navy rain jacket and leather hiking boots. He smiled.

"What a surprise!" called Teddy. "Oh, dear—I hope there's nothing wrong with Daisy?"

"No. Not at all. "Everything is fine." He leaned back inside and pulled out a gleaming double-barrelled gun, weaving it through his right arm like a farmer out for crows.

Teddy called cheerfully. "You don't need that here, it's perfectly safe."

"I have no doubt." Mr. Silva walked up to the stoop, and waited. The mood grew increasingly somber. Something ugly was sucking safety from the air.

Teddy said, "If you don't mind, we have to get something out of here and it's rather private."

Silva nodded. "My fazenda is also private. It will make the coffee a much better home."

"Your what?"

"My fazenda. My home."

All at once Teddy's spine understood what her brain did not. Fear grabbed her shoulders and slapped her in the jaw. The strength drained entirely from her arms and the keys fell to the soft earth by the stoop. She did not move to pick them up.

"Actually, sir"—Aurie shifted his weight—"I don't think you need to use that gun. If you just put it down, we'll be glad to leave the area immediately."

"How charming you are, Dr. Scholl."

Teddy blustered, "Y-you killed Leo."

Silva frowned. "Many things happen that are out of our control."

"If it was an accident, just say so. Everyone'll understand."

"There are no accidents, my dear, only destiny—and the greater causes that are larger than ourselves." He waved the gun. "You have already been especially troublesome with your ramblings these past days. Now please oblige me and move away from the door."

Teddy stepped off the stoop and smashed the key fob into

the soft earth. She pressed hard with her foot. "You're making a terrible mistake. You'll never get away, even if you kill us both."

Aurie persisted, "If you let us go, sir, you can have anything you like."

"I know that, Dr. Scholl." Silva lifted the gun and aimed it at Aurie's chest. "And what I would like in a moment is for a big strong man like you to help me load the coffee in my van. But first we have the other business to attend to." He gestured to Teddy with the twin barrels. "Both of you, get in your car, please."

Pressing hard on the keys, Teddy pivoted toward the door. "The door's locked, I don't think we can open it for you." She pivoted again, pressing harder. "Aurie, do you have the key?"

"I don't have the key."

Mr. Silva smiled indulgently. "It's no matter, really. Dr. Faber gave us his. Now please get in the car. Wait! Dr. Scholl, your trailer is a nuisance. We'll leave it here."

Aurie didn't know whether to move or not. "Do you want me to undo it?"

"Yes—Teddy, no!" Silva aimed the gun. "Stay right beside him. Move when he does. That's it, yes. Please think smartly, dear."

Together Teddy and Aurie walked to the car where he uncoupled the trailer. They waited.

"Now go with him, Teddy. Drag it to the bushes."

They dragged the trailer into the tall ferns and stood listening to the soft rain as it kissed the forest floor. Teddy quickly glanced at Aurie for cues. Alarmed, he stared back wide-eyed, begging her for good behavior.

Silva approached the Saab. "Now both get in the car. Dr. Scholl, you will drive."

They climbed in and at the same instant Silva slipped in behind Aurie. Between the bucket seats he trained the blue-black barrels on Teddy. Aurie looked in the mirror for instructions.

"Follow the road on farther. We need to ride a bit."

Aurie started down the track, switching the wipers on intermittent against the mist. When they reached the ashen gravel Silva said, "Turn right."

Teddy barely turned her head. "You can't just take the coffee. It has patents."

Silva smiled. "Would it surprise you to know the identical work is going on in Brazil? The similarities are uncanny."

"But people will boycott it, there'll be trouble."

"No, dear. What you need to understand about coffee, is that at special moments in time, a champion has always come forward to liberate it from the rapacious few. In the tenth century Baba Budan smuggled seven seeds to Mecca in his belly button, in the eighteenth Monsieur de Clieu shared his water rations with a single potted *arabica* to get it to the New World." He fell silent.

"B—"

"Now," he said, "we shall have the century of Brazil."

They drove through maple bog for several miles and then started climbing through a plantation of twenty-year-old Douglas fir. "Turn here," barked Silva. He pointed to a rough logging road gouged into the sandstone.

Sharply Aurie twisted the steering wheel and they wound their way up the hill. The road was a ridge-runner—in and out of several sandstone crests, then opening into a clear-cut, beyond which was a sandy blond logging road traversing a steep grade. The clear-cut was about five years old—with maples the size of Christmas trees and spindly alders ready to bud. "Turn here," Silva said.

"Where are we going?" asked Aurie.

"I told you, for a drive."

Aurie shifted down to second and turned uphill. The car sung tenor, happy in its work. They climbed a mile to the summit. Aurie stopped. At the crest was a breathtaking view of the neighboring hilltops. "Go on," urged Silva.

They ran the crest, and then dipped, ridge-running again in S-curves along the side of an old glacial dike. At each outer curve the view was spectacular, at each inner one, a waterfall. The air was chillier up here. They wove in and out for several miles and the road dipped lowland again. This made Silva fidget. At a fork, he burst out, "Turn here!"

Aurie turned, and again they climbed. Silva seemed pacified. The rain was still soft, and raggy strips of cloud clung to trees. They rode upward a mile. Finally they rounded a curve and came out into a new, naked clear-cut. From the open hillside they could see salt water forty miles away. Navy islands, gray sea, rain-laden clouds like flannel sheets.

"Stop!"

Aurie jammed on the brakes.

"Get out, both of you."

They climbed out and stood in the soft rain. Below, the skinned hillside fell away, a battlefield of raw orange stumps and piled slash.

"Teddy, walk to the edge, please."

She obeyed.

"Now look at the ridge over there."

She looked across the valley to the next nubby slope.

"Do you see the hill after that?"

"Yes."

"On the other side of that is Index. If you walk down this hill and up the next, you will make it back to Index in three or four hours."

Teddy blinked. Silva must have been in a really stupid Boy Scout troop; if she walked this way for three hours, all she would be was lost—three hours closer to Canada. "Are you sure?" she asked.

"Yes."

Aurie cried, "Teddy—"

"Dr. Scholl, get in the car."

"We can't leave her here."

Teddy peeked at the men. Silva was holding the shotgun to Aurie's chest. "It's regrettable," Silva said, "but I cannot deal with you both."

"Then leave *me*," Aurie said.

"That I could, but you must carry my pots."

"She's not dressed for this." Aurie jabbed into his pocket, and Silva cocked the gun. Instantly Aurie pulled out his hand. "May I give her my hat?"

"Slowly."

From his jacket Aurie pulled out a rust-colored watchcap and held it up.

"Toss it to her, please."

The knit cap landed several feet in front of Teddy and she looked at Silva to see if she was allowed to pick it up.

"Leave it there." Silva turned to Aurie. "Dr. Scholl, it's time to leave. Don't worry about Teddy, she'll be in Index in three hours."

Slowly Aurie walked to the car. He stood in the gap of the open door, alarm written large on his face. Rain peppered his glasses and a drop had formed on the end of his nose. "Teddy, you do know—"

"Dr. Scholl!"

He got in the car. Silva, too, climbed in, diagonally in back of Aurie. He rested the gun barrels on the curve of the bucket seat, against Aurie's forearm.

The car rolled forward and Teddy nodded unseeing at the glossy windshield to let Aurie know she wouldn't walk overland. She couldn't see his face, but waved goodbye anyway.

The Saab turned around, rear tires jutting over the side of the slope as Aurie maneuvered back and forth. He disappeared down the hill.

16

Light rain daubed her head and Teddy bent down to pick up Aurie's hat. It was cashmere and soft, the rust color perfect for his eyes and horn-rimmed glasses. Someone who had loved him had bought it, and briefly she was happy that Jennifer had never let him venture more than ten miles from the mall.

She pulled the cap far down on her head and buttoned the velvet trenchcoat to her chin. Down the hill the brown Saab disappeared around a curve. She tucked her hands in her pockets and looked the other way, up the road. It had a slight upward grade, which seemed an unlikely route to civilization.

In the Saab's tracks, she trounced down the logging road, taking inventory of her condition. Her nose was cold—she sniffed—that was okay. But her shoulders were cold, and that was not. She wriggled her back. The waterproofing from the dry cleaner's was not holding up well. But she had known all along that real raincoats weren't velvet.

Striding in giant steps, she glanced down at the clear-cut. It really was very recent—orange oxidation on raw stumps. She turned west to look again at faraway Puget Sound, if only to get her bearings. The entire sky was leaden gray and low enough to touch. Her watch said twelve-thirty.

For fifteen minutes she walked downhill, consciously keeping her pace under exertion level. Sweat began to form under the rim of the watchcap and she folded it back. A shiver ran down her spine, so she turned up her collar. Body heat was everything. And Aurie, he was everything, too.

Aurie? The thought astonished her. She strode down the hill, letting him settle in. What was all this? She objected to so many things about him—his values, his narcissism; she didn't even like his cooking. But Marmee was right: for whatever reason, she felt most alive in his field of vision.

She stumbled down to the first intersection. In the blond sand two sets of Saab tracks turned right. She, too, turned right, and trudged ahead. Her shoulders were very cold and very wet, and there was no correction to be made for them. Her toes were also cold, her feet were wet.

The road rose again and she tried not to work hard as she climbed. She wiped rain and sweat off her forehead with her sleeve. She took off Aurie's cap, and a chill ran through her hair. She put it back on and kept walking. All would be fine— just fine—until she had to stop tonight.

After a while the road leveled off and she could see ahead the five or six ridges she would be traversing in the next five or six hours. Fear knotted her stomach. She walked.

For ten minutes she trudged ahead, keeping a careful balance between chill and sweat. She paced on methodically, trying to remember hiking songs.

Far away a roaring noise—like the sound of a waterfall— rushed in on a rogue wind. Suddenly behind was pandemonium. She turned around to see a monstrous chrome grille the size of a building. "Peterbilt." She stared for a single frozen second, then jumped off the road.

The truck roared past, the gale sweeping her nearly from her feet. The cab was metallic brown with orange pin-striping. The trailer behind was crested high with a tight load of Douglas fir—big stuff, with fresh orange butts and peeled orange scars. Behind the trailer was a smaller pup trailer, also crested above the bunks. The truck downshifted and blasted air. Finally it came to a stop.

"Jesus, lady!" Down from the cab a heavy-set man dropped to the earth. He wore jeans and red suspenders and a hickory striped workshirt. The suspenders were printed "Deming Log Show" and bulged hugely over his belly.

Teddy ran to meet him. In his eyes she saw what she looked like—poster child for the homeless, the Sasquatch's daughter. "Please, can I get in?"

Openmouthed, he gestured to the towering cab. "Other side."

She crossed in front of the growling grille, half-afraid it would lunge. She climbed the two hidden steps and tumbled into the plush chair. All of a sudden she couldn't speak. The cab was cushioned and cozy, Tammy Wynette was on the radio. In the open cooler between the seats were grapes, crackers, thermos, chocolate, a thick-crusted sandwich.

"Lady?" He looked at her face and turned the heat on high. She worked to stifle her tears.

"Lady, what's the matter?"

"Can we call the police?" Teddy heaved. "A man with a sh-shotgun left me here about an hour ago. He's got my friend, he's already killed my brother-in-law."

"No shit?" The driver picked up his cellular. "What's your name?"

She exhaled. "Teddy Morelli."

"I'm Wiley."

"Wiley."

"Closest cops are Sultan, cellular's out of range." He dropped the cellular and picked up his CB. "Let me call my show." He pressed "send."

"Yo. Grabber?"

There was static and Teddy could barely make out: "Grabber. Whats?"

"Grabber, this is Coyote. I'm on the back side of Ragged Ridge and I got a woman here who wants us to call the cops. Says a guy left her up here, he's got a shotgun."

Loud static. There was silence and Grabber transmitted again. "This ain't about Yost and all, is it?"

With pained expression, Wiley muffled the mike against his heavy thigh. "You don't happen to date a guy named Yost Wister do you?"

Pitifully she sniffed. "We're from Seattle."

Wiley held the mike to his mouth. "She's from Seattle."

"Seattle," said Grabber, and signed off.

Teddy pulled a seatbelt from the high cab wall over her shoulder. "Could we hurry, please? I'm really worried about my friend."

Wiley stopped her hands. "Don't put that on. If the brakes go, you want to be able to jump out fast." He worked the gears. "Your friend's a guy, huh?"

"He's a doctor in Seattle. He does the Seahawks' knees."

"No kidding?" Wiley checked his mirrors. "What's your name again?"

"Teddy."

Wiley pressed pedals and air blasted near the tires. "The guy with the shotgun, he really kill your brother-in-law?"

"Yes."

"Then where's your doctor? We should have the cops show up there." Wiley rolled forward.

Teddy sat upright in the button-tufted armchair. The cab was astonishingly high above the road. Down by her ankle, through an oval window, gravel zipped by in a blur. "Both of them are down at a greenhouse on Road 7099. It's off in the woods and the only thing marking it are two concrete stanchions. I can try to take you there. No, wait! See those tire prints? Just follow those."

Wiley shifted and picked up the CB mike again. "Then what? We get shot at when we get there?"

"I don't know. Please hurry."

Wiley held the mike to his mouth and repeated the information to Grabber, angel on an unseen hillside. Wiley hung up and looked at the clock on his jetlike dashboard. "Somebody's going to have to pull the cops off their lunch in Sultan. They aren't going to like it.'' He glanced at Teddy. ''Want me to just follow the tracks on down there, and we hang back, wait for the cops?''

''Yes, please. That would be great.''

They rolled down hill, Wiley maneuvering the fifty-ton trailers as if they were nothing more than red wagons. At each turn-off the Saab's fresh prints directed them. In only a few minutes they were down in the maple boglands on the pale ashen gravel. Mosses glowed emerald in the rain. Teddy sat forward. ''It's around here somewhere. This is very close.''

''Gravel's too packed to follow tracks.'' Wiley turned his wipers up a notch. ''You're going to have to tell me when to stop.'' He rolled forward slowly, watching her face. ''Make sure we stop before the shotgun.''

She gulped. ''I'm trying.''

''We make a lot of noise in this truck.''

''I'm trying.''

They rolled down the gravel, rounding a broad curve. Up ahead, a black van was parked to one side.

''Stop! That's his van. There're the stanchions, see?'' She pointed farther down the road to the stubby concrete pillars.

''Gotcha.'' Wiley shot out blasts from the air brakes and the truck stood humming in the road. ''I hate to tell you this, lady, but there's no telling when the police'll show up.''

Teddy bit her lip.

He loosened his gear stick. ''What's the bad guy's name?''

''Renato Silva.''

''He's dealing? Or your brother-in-law?''

''Neither. This is about some coffee.''

''No shit? I thought you were going to tell me meth.'' Wiley batted the gear stick again. ''So Renato is going to off your doctor friend because you guys know about the brother-in-law?''

''Aah!'' Teddy threw open the door and jumped to the ground. She trotted down the gravel while behind her the truck shot loud air. Wiley called, "Wait. Let me come with ya." He padded after her, panting. "You gotta tell me, really, you guys legit?"

She walked faster. "I don't know what that means."

They paced silently down the road, Wiley puffing red-faced to keep up. At Silva's van they became quiet and Teddy looked in. On the driver's seat was a pair of men's black dress shoes. Oddly, there were no coffee plants in the van.

Teddy whispered, "I wonder what the shoes are for?"

"They the doctor's?"

"No."

Wiley tapped the window. "That's a good sign."

They crossed the road over to the stanchions and padded down the two-track. Breathing heavily, Wiley pressed her into the undergrowth on the side. "Let's stay out of sight."

Slowly—a stone's throw from the two-track—they made their way through the maple trees, over the ferny hummocks that signaled long-ago logging. Teddy led the way, hopping between quiet spots of damp earth. Up ahead was the hulking green crustacean butting from the hill. A sudden whiff of wind brought the urban smell of Wiley's truck. She sniffed again and it was gone.

Wiley grabbed her arm. "Just a minute," he panted. "I need to catch my breath." He leaned over red-faced behind the salal and rested his hands on his knees. "We shouldn't do this. I hate to leave my truck."

Annoyed at his sluggishness, she poked her head up to look. "I still can't see anything."

"Duck!" He pressed on her head.

She squatted instantly. "What?"

Wiley pointed in a direction that seemed unrelated, far to the right of the greenhouse. "Is that your guy?"

She peeked from behind the salal to make out Silva's navy rain jacket. "Yes. What's he doing?"

"Can't tell. Let's go closer." Wiley tiptoed ahead, suddenly agile as an Indian. Crouched, he padded over the damp earth, making no more noise than the maples. Twenty yards closer he dropped behind a rotten fir trunk. They both peeked over to see Silva fussing around the generator shed.

Wiley flared his nostrils. "That's diesel."

"I thought it was your truck."

"My truck smells like *cooked* diesel."

Silva suddenly looked their way.

"Don't move."

They held perfectly still and after a moment Teddy craned up again. "What's he doing?"

Silva worked unhappily on the spigot of the fuel tank, vexation twisting his face. On top of the low shed rested his shotgun. "I don't see Aurie," she said. "He must be in the greenhouse."

Wiley wiped sweat from his face, and answered somberly. "The Quonset door's *open*."

"What does that mean?"

Wiley didn't answer.

Silva moved to the side and they saw that he was holding a lusterless beer can under the diesel fuel line. He was clearly frustrated with the slowness of the stream and after a moment he poured a bit of fuel around the edge of the shed. He again held his beer can under the leak. He was very annoyed.

"Wiley, what's he done to Aurie in the greenhouse? Do you think he's okay?"

Wiley scowled. "Your Aurie ain't in the greenhouse. Your Aurie's in deep shit."

"Where is he?"

"Don't you see what Renato's doing?"

"He's pouring gasoline around the shed."

"Diesel. Works just as well."

"A-Aurie's in there!" She buried her head, whimpering behind the log.

"Shotgun's on the shed roof," said Wiley. "Is that all he's got?"

She willed her voice to work. "I don't know. I think so."

She raised her head. "Wiley, help. Can't we do something? Make him come *this* way. Anything."

Wiley lifted himself heavily into a squat. He looked around the forest floor, then back toward the road. "I'm better in my truck."

"Let's go."

Crouching low, they ran toward the road. It was much farther than she remembered and Wiley had to stop several times to rest. Finally she burst out onto the gravel to see the huge Peterbilt purring farther down, ready to take on all comers. Teddy reached it first and climbed up the steps to scan for police cars, for any cars at all. "What if they don't come?"

"Get in," Wiley puffed.

Obediently Teddy climbed into the cab and slammed the door. "Wiley, something's really wrong. Renato should have just taken the coffee and left."

"You know what?" Wiley batted his gear stick. "Renato is going to make his getaway in that van. That's why he left his shoes." He shot out air and the truck sped down the gravel. "I don't think my rig'll fit through the stanchions."

"Maybe we can honk from the road."

"Like hell." Steering straight toward the stanchions, Wiley suddenly swerved the wheel and gunned the engine.

"Wiley!"

Without warning they plowed into the underbrush. Saplings disappeared under the grille. Teddy held onto the armrests as if they were tenure track.

Suddenly Wiley veered back onto the lane, jouncing in the seat. He was humming and alert, clearly in his element. He swatted gears and they sped forward loudly. "Okay, if he starts with his shotgun, you drop down on the floor, you hear?"

"Look, there he is!"

Not far down the two-track, Silva was walking backward, coming their way, awkwardly sweeping a huge fir bough across the track. When he heard the Peterbilt behind him, he

dropped the branch and began to run. He was a clumsy runner, even with empty arms.

"He left the gun!" shouted Wiley. "It's still on the shed."
He was gleeful.

Silva clumped awkwardly down the road when suddenly
his shoe flew off and landed in the ferns. He kicked off the
other one and ran efficiently.

Teddy squeaked, "Those were Aurie's shoes!" It came out
as a question.

Stocking-footed, Silva sprinted into the clearing in front of
the Quonset hut and looked off toward the generator shed at
his shotgun.

Wiley scowled. "If Renato goes after his gun, I'm going
have to run him down." He turned. "You hear what I'm
saying?"

Teddy gritted her teeth, ready to watch Silva disappear under the grille.

Wiley reached up and tugged his horn chain, subtly con-
veying to Silva exactly what he had told her. Silva ran two
more steps, then—finessed by the horn message—veered
away from the generator, making a beeline for the greenhouse.

"Ha!" shouted Wiley. "We got him!" He jounced happily
in the seat.

Silva ran into the greenhouse and slammed the door. Wiley
hit the gas and aimed at the flat front wall.

"Wiley!"

"Gotta keep him inside." He tooted the horn and shifted
gears for maximum effect. The noise was deafening.

"Wiley, be careful!" Teddy clutched the armrests, her
knuckles white. Wiley rolled to a stop inches from the greenhouse, then shifted gears. "Got him."

Suddenly the door swung open and Silva clubbed Wiley's
grille with a long steel pipe.

"Fucking bastard." Wiley blared the horn.

Silva hacked defiantly.

Wiley tapped the gas and inched his grille into the sheet-metal wall; Silva banged in rage. "Cut it out, you bastard!"

Wiley tapped again and the building rumbled. Silva banged furiously with his steel pipe. This time Wiley shifted gears, blared his horn, and hit the gas pedal.

In slow motion, the corrugated metal roof began to swell before their eyes, emitting a sound like a screaming pig. Rising like bread dough, the building rumbled and thundered, protesting against the new shape Wiley demanded. Silva glanced back, then dropped his pipe and disappeared. Wiley nudged more. "Take that, you bastard."

The front wall of the Quonset hut was molded into Wiley's grille. No one would be using the door for quite a while. Wiley grunted, satisfied. Wiggling the gear stick, he relieved the brakes. "Go get the shotgun!" he barked. "Quick."

Teddy hopped down and dashed across the clearing. She grabbed the shotgun from the top of the shed, astonished at its weight. "Aurie, we're here."

He banged. "Get me out!"

"I'm trying!"

She hobbled back across the yard, anxiously scanning the Quonset hut for windows or doors she may have missed. There were no windows, only a new bowed opening low along the side wall.

Reaching the truck, she handed the shotgun up to Wiley and climbed in. Wiley checked the safety and stood the gun in the space between the seats. "Much better. Lock your door."

"What's Silva doing?"

"I don't know. Dark in there." Picking up his CB mike, he called again for Grabber. Static was the response. "Out of range." He punched 911 into the cellular, but to no effect. He fiddled with the CB dials. "Come on, Grabber." Still only static.

Nothing was visible inside the greenhouse. Wiley gunned

the engine and tortured the building just for effect. "Where are the fucking police?"

Teddy rolled down the window and shouted, "Aurie, don't worry. The police are coming."

"He can't hear you."

"He wants out of the shed. Can I go try?"

"No, stay here. We don't know if Renato's got a gun, or if there's a back door to the greenhouse."

Teddy looked at the fat ventilation stacks sprouting from the unseen back wall of the greenhouse. "There couldn't be. It'd make the building less secure." She turned around to see if help was arriving. Behind her was a sheer wall of orange fir butts.

Frustrated, she used the side mirror to view the dirt road. Wiley sat fiddling with his CB. "Come on, Grabber."

They waited, the truck humming happily beneath, ready for its next task. "What do you think he'll do?" she asked.

Wiley gunned the engine again and jerked the horn. "I don't know. I don't like this." He checked his mirror. "Where *are* the fucking police?"

"I'm going to get Aurie out."

"No, you're not. Stay here."

"But there's no back door to the greenhouse. And the side holes are too low. He's stuck!"

"Lady, I said stay here."

"Wiley, I just remembered." She pointed to the floor of the cab. "The key to the generator shed is right under me, next to the front wheel. If you can hold still, I'll climb under and dig it out. It will take about six seconds."

"Jesus, lady!"

"Wiley, we have his gun. It's the only one he brought."

He touched the stock. "That doesn't mean *I* know how to use it!"

"Please, Wiley, let me try." She opened the door and dropped down to the ground, peeking under the massive mud flap to a tire the size of a Lazy-Boy. She poked her head back into the cab. "Don't move the truck, okay?"

"Laa-deee." He grabbed his wheel.

She dropped to her belly, and poked her head under the truck. The noise was deafening.

She wriggled back out and lay with her cheek in the dirt—if she stood up again, Wiley would yell at her. Taking a deep breath, she bellied under the roaring truck, clawing with hands and feet. The firewood stoop was dead center under the engine. She slithered to the right, and found the rough circle she had pressed in the mud. With her index finger she dug the wet earth. The key fob came easily.

Clutching the fob, she scooted backward under the truck, slithering far out, flat on her belly, before she tried to stand. She ran across the clearing to the generator shed. "Aurie, I'm here!" she shouted over the noise.

"Amloy" was on the generator padlock; the key turned as if jumping. The door banged open and Aurie emerged hunched and blinking. His expression was vague and far away.

"Aurie, are you okay?"

He looked strangely at her lips and didn't answer.

"Are you *okay*?"

"I hear noises," he shouted.

Far away a siren wailed. "It's the police!"

From the truck Wiley tooted his horn and she glanced over to the Peterbilt. Wiley was pointing to a spot on the sheer cliff behind the greenhouse.

"Aurie, look!" she said.

High above, Silva was scrambling up the bank, using both hands to climb.

17

She stood with a Sultan policeman watching Silva's navy rain jacket grow smaller on the hill. The cop frowned as he called for dogs and backup, mildly annoyed that he'd be outside in the rain all afternoon.

Scowling into the transmitter, the cop tried to explain to someone far away the arrangement of greenhouse and looming cliff, and how Silva had shoved a plank out a ventilator hole to reach the cliff to climb. He listened to a woolly reply, then called across the roof of the cruiser to Aurie. "He got another weapon?"

"Not to my knowledge, Officer. But I'd be careful."

The cop turned away to avoid ridicule.

A second cop trotted up to Aurie and handed him one of his overpriced French walking shoes. "Can't find the other one, sir. You'll have to wait for the dog."

Over by the Quonset hut Wiley buffed his grille with a chamois, muttering endearments and sympathy. When he was finished, he walked the truck for inspection, tugging the binders on his load. Finally he ambled over to the police car.

"How's your truck?" asked Teddy.

"Couple of gouges. Most of it'll polish out." He turned to the policeman. "I'm way late, I gotta get moving. If you need me, I'm on my way to the sort yard in Everett."

The cop pointed to Wiley's name and address on his clipboard. "And you'll be home tonight, sir?"

"Yeah."

"Thank you very much. Appreciate your cooperation."

"Yeah, well . . ." He was too polite to finish. He climbed into the cab and fired up the Peterbilt, deftly backing the twin trailers across the clearing. He tooted softly and raised a hand to Teddy. Teddy raised one in return.

Shivering under the aluminum space blanket, she turned toward the impossibly bent greenhouse. It was high-humped now, like a well-fed Bactrian camel, with airy bell-shaped openings on both sides. In front of the bashed-in facade lay a new concrete terrace. The door was still open and looked as if it alone was propping up the front wall. Her teeth chattered and she went around and stood next to Aurie for the body heat. He was using the open back door of the police car as a mobile office, talking on his phone.

She moved in close, shivering; Silva scrambled farther up the hill. "Why didn't he just take the coffee and leave?"

Aurie stepped away, gesturing distractedly with his phone. "Go see in the greenhouse."

She glanced first at the policemen. Both were leaning against the car, admiring Silva's technique on a particularly nasty gravel slide. She padded across the clearing and entered the Quonset hut, waiting for her eyes to adjust to the light.

Long plywood tables were shoved together toward the back and cockeyed clusters of growlights hovered like coolie hats in a storm. Mixed in with the coolie hats were pungent dried marijuana shrubs hanging upside down from the rafters. She glanced at the back wall. Jutting from the round high vent hole was a tired gray plank, across which Silva had climbed onto a ferny hummock. She couldn't find the coffee.

Walking was impossible. Every inch of floor was covered with tipped-over silver-leafed plants, their black potting soil strewn around like bird food. Teddy knelt down and righted one of the gray-colored bushes. It was coffee—more or less—

but the big veined leaves were curled under and winter-white, like the mouths of old people without their teeth.

"Miss?" A policeman stood in the space beside the door. "You got to come out of there, it's not safe. We don't know what-all they'll cordon off."

Teddy plucked a withered leaf and folded it discreetly under her space blanket. She trotted across the clearing to Aurie and hid behind him to examine her stolen leaf. Turning it over she found a tidy silver web. She poked gently and a spiderlike insect scurried sideways.

"Aurie, what are they?"

"Silver mites? I don't know. Renato called them *pragas*. He was so mad he knocked the pots off the table." Aurie looked away to indicate he was busy.

She held up the leaf. "But this could be saved. Most of the plants still have *some* life."

Aurie brandished the phone aggressively, shaking his head.

"Well, at least the seeds!"

"Teddy, think about it: Leo took the caffeine out, remember? This stuff is going to be ungrowable with no protection from bugs." He punched his phone. "Coffee makes caffeine for a reason."

She looked up. "So you think the whole idea of chocolate coffee is a bust?"

"I don't know." Aurie listened to his phone ring and would not meet her eyes. "But clearly they're not ready for prime time." Alertly he broke off. "This is Dr. Scholl. I'm calling about Mrs. Vanger's results."

"Poor Leo." Her words rose like a sigh.

Aurie was avoiding her, using doctoring not to deal with the now. She waited for him to finish on the phone. He noticed her waiting, and dropped into the back seat, sliding all the way to the other side. She slid in beside him.

Through the woods two white police cars rolled up slowly, their light bars flashing like a Wal-Mart closeout sale. Aurie bent his head to watch. She watched, too.

"Are you okay?" she asked.

"Fine."

"It must have been awful in the shed."

"I just canceled tomorrow's surgeries, I was *supposed* to do an arthroscopic on House Berry." Quietly he added, "Brantley said he'd take it."

"Aurie, I'm so sorry."

"Ah, yes. That old familiar rhyme."

"You're angry with me."

"No! It's not your fault." He wouldn't look at her. "I should have known better than to get mixed up in this in the first place."

"I'm sorry you're so angry."

"Everything's fine, *okay*?" He exhaled loudly. And he still wouldn't look at her.

On Saturday morning she left a message on his voice mail, the third in two days. The machine beeped and she began cheerily: "Hello, again. I guess you heard Marmee's back. She and Daisy are making sole Parmesan for dinner tonight and I'm in the middle of rolling gnocchi." She paused, deciding that mention of marinated crab legs would sound over-eager. "We all hope you can come, we're very anxious to see you—especially me.

"We plan to gather at six and sit down around seven. The Oliveris are coming, and Carlo. Carlo's going to tape Louie Oliveri doing his Miss Asia act so he can send it to his host family in Brazil." She paused again. "Hope you can make it tonight."

By six he had not called back, so for dinner she slipped on a red sweater of Daisy's, hoping it would distract the mood-sniffing elders from her disappointment. She ran a comb through her hair and went down to the kitchen. Daisy and Marmee were working at the counter, the powdered light from the lake floating around like grace.

". . . the most amazing thing," said Marmee, "is that each island has separate species you can tell apart—its own tortoises, and finches, and booby birds. People who live there know exactly where an animal is from."

Marmee's perfect skin was a buttery tan and the corners of her eyes had eerie white sun-squints. All her Seattle succulence had been broiled away and around her head floated a vague cloud of new experience. "Blue-footed booby," she said, "isn't that wonderful?"

"Blue-footed booby," repeated Daisy.

"They also said they used the Galapagos tortoise's head for the movie *E.T.* Did you know that?" Marmee's Italian accent was overlaid with a bit of Oxbridge lilt—there had been English people on the trip.

Daisy snipped parsley. "All I remember about *E.T.* is he was too lizardy for merchandising."

"Teodora." Marmee handed Teddy a short tumbler packed with carrot and celery sticks. "Bring these out to Carlo in the living room. He keeps coming after my flat beans."

She took the tumbler and Marmee added, "Your sweater looks nice. Maybe he'll call tomorrow—if you go to church in the morning."

Teddy found Carlo standing in front of the T.V., watching a homemade tape of Daisy sewing brand-new Arthur Rabbitstein onto his stand. "Leo," she was saying, "Please stop."

The unseen cameraman replied, "But we need to get your backside, dear. There's hardly anything else that looks like that."

Carlo quickly turned off the tape and plucked some carrot sticks. "Thanks, T." He flicked his brown ponytail off his shoulder and smiled with chipmunk eyes; he had already forgotten his outburst the other day. To the kitchen, he called, "Hey, Daisy, are there any clean tapes we can use?"

Daisy appeared in the front hall. "Tape over anything, Carlo, it doesn't matter. As a matter of fact, you can have the whole camera, if you like."

Carlo's eyes widened to portholes. "To keep?"

"Sure. I'll never use it. It was just something Leo brought home." She disappeared into the kitchen.

"Wow! Thanks."

A few moments later Marmee came out, wiping her hands on a towel. Like the rest of them, she stared at his bejeweled nostril. "Carlo, offer the camera back to her in a few months, just in case."

"Yes, ma'am."

As she left she called back over her shoulder. "I found my lost garnet if you want it for your other"—she tapped her face—"nose."

"Thanks, Ma!"

Teddy watched Carlo set up the camera, then went back to the kitchen to find Daisy telling about her week. "It was like your frittata, Marmee. She put in big chucks of crab, and it was really good, but that night I dreamed that there was a bunch of us with long arms were in a wire cage, and we were all *furious* because someone had left us there without any food, so all we could do was bite off little bits from each other's bodies. We all just *hated* it, and were really irritable, but we knew we had to cooperate."

Teddy gestured to the planked sole. "Gee, Daisy, you're going to have to stop eating flesh altogether."

"Oh, I've never had any problem with plain fish. In fish dreams, I'm just always surprised to be pulled from the water, then the dream dissolves."

There was a noise from the front of the house and they looked out to see three members of the Oliveri family standing on the porch. Red beret jaunty, Mrs. Oliveri caught sight of Marmee through the etched glass. She rushed in.

"Maria!"

"Irene!" Marmee hugged her friend. "How are the children? How is everything?"

Teddy stood with Daisy in the kitchen doorway watching the two old friends hug and talk. As she rested against the jamb, tears swelled in her eyes and she could feel—palpably, beside her—Daisy's gray cloud diffuse a bit and clarify.

Handsome little Louie Oliveri held his garment bag over his head and made quick polite greetings to all. Then he dashed into the living room to be with Carlo.

Mr. Oliveri spotted the sisters in the doorway and walked back to the kitchen cradling a bottle of red wine and a pound of Oliveri coffee beans.

Teddy breathed in the rich Oliveri smell—the smell of safety, and Seattle, and morning kitchens. Mr. Oliveri smiled with his perfect white teeth. "Delizia, Teodora, you girls get prettier everytime I see you. Teodora. My mother's name was Teodora."

Teddy smiled. "Is that right?"

"Her brother was Giustino. After the mosaics at Ravenna."

"I must see them sometime."

"You must see them sometime." He held up the pound of coffee and murmured conspiratorially, "I left Fazenda da Silva out of the mix."

Smiling, Teddy grabbed a handful of carrot sticks and wandered around back, through the sunroom, to be with the boys in the living room. Wiry little Louie took off his jacket to casually display a ripped set of shoulder muscles under a black tank top. Ignoring his gooseflesh, he stood with his hands in his back pockets, admiring Carlo's new video goods.

Her brother gestured to Louie's blatant display. "Serious pumpatude, bro."

"Oh, that." Louie glanced down, having forgotten it was there. "Yeah, I had to lay it on for the Asia Contest. My dress straps kept falling off."

Teddy cocked an eyebrow. "Louie, you don't think you might be gay, do you?"

Louie rubbed his biscuited abs. "I sure hope so. It's a great way to pick up chicks."

"Which reminds me, Teddy." Carlo struck a pose, planting his feet apart, and crossing his arms high over his chest. "Tell him women don't stand like this, with their legs apart. You look like the Jolly Green Giant."

"It's attitude, bro!"

Carlo pleaded. "Tell him he's wrong!"

Teddy shook her head. "I agree with Louie. We just spent the last three decades making it okay for women to stand however they want. What you're asking is how a drag queen would stand to look like a woman."

"See! See!"

"Well," Carlo cooed falsetto. "I don't think it's very feminine."

" 'Tis."

" 'Tisn't."

" 'Tis."

"I'm leaving," said Teddy.

Carlo went to the stereo. "What tune-age you want, bro?

They sat down to antipasto—Alaska crab legs marinated in red wine vinegar and butter, and an eggplant-carrot semplice—chilled stew in individual casseroles.

"Maria," asked Mr. Oliveri. "What was your one chief impression of the Galapagos?"

"One? I would say that Galapagos shows you what we've done wrong in making friends on the planet." She turned, "Teodora, *tenore*?"

"Tenor, it's a word."

"Tenor." Marmee continued. "The tenor of life in the Galapagos is so clement it makes you wish we hadn't violated so many species. The Galapagos animals are so little afraid of us—they never had a reason to be—it makes you sad that we have no friends among the species. Did you realize that? There are *no* other animals that even like to come near us."

"Dogs."

"Parasites."

"Dogs." She shrugged.

"Would you go again?" asked Mr. Oliveri.

"I want to see Egypt first."

Louie cleaned out his semplice in three bites. "That reminds me, Pop, I saw a shop today that'd have you totally flamed. Some kids are opening a coffee house by the U.— they keep geckos in a tank. Their house blend is called the Dancing Goat and they have another one, Wiener Victorious."

"*Vee*-ner Victorious," said Mr. Oliveri. "Go there. Those kids know what they're doing."

Louie swallowed. "What's 'vee-ner'?"

"Wien. Vienna. It's a reference to the Siege of Vienna when a man named Kolschitsky got five hundred bags of green coffee the Turks left behind. He opened a shop and nobody would drink Turkish coffee because it was so bitter. So he added cream and honey, and people came."

"Then what's 'Dancing Goat'?"

Oliveri shrugged. "That would be little Kaldi the Goatherd who first discovered coffee. They say his goats ate red berries from a tree and they started to dance frisky. Kaldi tried the berries himself and liked the effect."

"Bonus." Louie glanced across the table. "Teddy, will you do my makeup for me after dinner? I can't put on eye goop without blinking."

"I hope you brought your own eye goop. I don't have any right now."

Daisy brightened. "You can use mine. I also have some stretchy combs that will hold the tiara on when you dance."

Louie said flatly, "I don't *have* the tiara."

"But Teddy said you won."

"It was protested by the guy who got second place, because I'm not Asian."

"That's true." His father nodded. "You're *not* Asian."

"But, Pop!" Calmly Louie put down his fork. "Pop, they were all perfectly down with it before the contest. Nobody cared until I won."

"And you're surprised?"

"No, I'm bitter," said Louie. "Everybody rags about diversity, but as soon as you start mixing it up, they all scurry back to their own little holes."

"It's people being people, Louie. Now you know."

After antipasto, Marmee brought out the sole Parmesan, gnocchi in a blue bowl, more bread, and flat beans sauted in garlic and olive oil. "Mega, Mom," said Carlo.

Daisy surveyed the food. "Leo likes gnocchi."

They stared at their plates.

"I mean," Daisy said, "Leo *liked* gnocchi. Didn't he, Marmee?"

"Leo liked all my food. Leo was a good boy."

"What did they do with that guy?" asked Carlo.

Marmee raised her chin. "Carlo, we're not going to talk about him here at the table."

Daisy piped, "It's okay, Marmee, I'm on my medication."

"Didn't he have kids and stuff?"

Marmee picked up the bread knife, glaring. "The policeman said they had all left for Brazil before they got there. Daisy, *cara*, could you go upstairs and get a handkerchief from my purse? I left it on your dresser."

"Sure, Marmee." Daisy pushed back her chair.

"Thank you, dear."

After Daisy left Carlo popped gnocchi in his mouth. "Sorry, Mom, but can I ask one question? Does anybody even know why he killed Leo in the first place?"

"To get his keys, bro."

"No, I mean, why can't you just wait and steal beans off the coffee tree when they're ready?"

Mr. Oliveri sipped water. "Hybrids don't reproduce, Carlo. AgroGene would have been in charge of all plant propagation."

"Cool."

Marmee cut angles of peasant bread and handed slices to those who wanted it. "Luigi, I want you to tell me something. If the two men struggled, and it was an accident with the scissors, why did this educated man keep stabbing my son-in-law over and over again. This is something Brazilian I don't understand?''

Mr. Oliveri frowned.

''Pop?'' Louie said, ''I was telling you, yesterday.''

''About what?''

''About the telenovela, *Diario de Rio*, the plot with the mistress and the scissors? Senhor Silva would have seen it—it was the best one the whole year. He would have realized if he just kept stabbing and stabbing it would start to look like a woman did it: 'un crime passional.' '' Louie swallowed. ''Except in the real one on TV, the guy got stabbed in the chest.''

They were silent a moment and Irene asked, ''Was Senhor Silva trying to incriminate Daisy, or Molly Thistle?''

''Maybe he didn't care.''

Louie skewered gnocchi. ''Pop, do you think the Pereira family knows Senhor Silva?''

Mr. Oliveri used his napkin. ''They certainly know *of* Mr. Silva. It's one of the oldest names in Minas Gerais.'' He glared at his son. ''You're not reading the sacks in the warehouse? Fazenda da Silva is one whole pallet back there.''

''I've seen it.'' Louie clutched his water glass. ''But what I still don't get is why he had to steal Leo's idea instead of just waiting for it. It'll go to Brazil first anyway—they're the best for yield.''

Mr. Oliveri cocked his head. ''Remember, Louie. If this ever works, AgroGene will want a lot of money, don't you think? The hybrid supplier could easily charge so much for each plant that loans are extended to pay. It's already a mess down there. I could imagine Silva seeing himself a patriot: the man who saves Brazil.''

''Do you think Senhor Silva was acting on his own? Or for the government or something?''

''Now, that's a good question. I guess we won't know that until we see what happens with his bail.''

"What do you mean, Pop?"

"Bail's been set at half a million. If someone comes up with it anonymously, it will tell whether he acted alone, or for a consortium."

"A consortium?"

"Of coffee growers."

Mrs. Oliveri buttered bread. "But there're still so many unanswered questions, Lou. I mean, how could Silva just walk into Leo's office in the first place? They're so security-conscious over there at the U." She frowned. "Unless they knew each other . . ."

"Um!" Teddy swallowed.

"Um, what?"

"I know why Leo let him in, and it wouldn't have mattered whether they knew each other or not."

"Why is that, doll?"

"Remember the little coffee tree that spilled in Leo's office the night of the murder—everyone said it wasn't R-19? Silva must have been carrying it under his arm. That would have made Leo open the door, wouldn't it?"

"Teodora, I bet you're right."

"Good call, T."

"Thank you. Thank you."

Mr. Oliveri spoke again, "Or maybe Leo th—"

Daisy came back with the handkerchief, and a small wrapped parcel. "Marmee, what's this?"

"It came today in the mail, but you were asleep."

Daisy set it aside. "I don't know anyone in Waterloo, California."

They finished the meal with talk of siblings and mutual friends and as they cleared plates, Teddy turned to Louie Oliveri. "If you want to get dressed upstairs, Daisy and I can come help you with your makeup."

"We gonna do this before coffee, Mrs. Morelli?"

"We'll bring coffee in the living room."

Louie darted upstairs and in a moment called down. "I'm ready for makeup, guys."

Daisy and Teddy went up to find Louie corseted into a tight red sequinned dress—a handsome young man vulnerably female from the neck down. It was both disconcerting and endearing.

"Come in here," said Teddy. "The light's better."

She sat him down on the dressing stool in Daisy's bathroom and worked close to his face under the florescent light. As she patted on foundation, blush, and eyeliner, he consciously looked away. They breathed moist air together and she forced herself remember that she had been twelve years old when he was born.

Daisy stood in the door. "Louie, you look good enough to eat."

"Bonus!"

Teddy painted on his luscious little mouth, happy that someone else had uttered her thought.

The smell of espresso wafted from below. Carlo called up the stairs. "We're ready down here."

Teddy dropped the makeup tools into the drawer. "You guys go on down, I need to make a phone call."

Daisy and Louie bounded down the stairs and Teddy picked up the bedroom extension. She punched in the number to Aurie's house and his machine picked up the call. She hung up.

"Teddy, hurry up. We're ready."

Everybody sat in the living room, Marmee pouring espresso into tiny cups. Daisy had pulled Arthur Rabbitstein from the corner and was hovering over him, pin cushion in hand.

"What are you doing?" asked Teddy.

"Look! Mungo sent it in the mail." She held out a rabbit snout, white and fluffy, tipped at the nose in the most urbane shade of pink velvet. "He wrote a note." She offered it and Teddy read:

Dear Miss Daisy,

I found the nose in my kit when I got here. Think it's still pretty frisky looking. Things look pretty good here in Stockton. I'm living with a friend east of town and he's in good with all the baseball community. I plan to put in with several athletic stores and batting cages, also with Stockton parks and rec. They are looking for a professional person to run LL this summer.

Teddy looked up. "What's LL?"
"Little League?"
"Oh."

I'm real sorry about leaving the cutting on you, but I feel it is in my best interest to quit Seattle until further notice. Please tell whoever starts cutting that they can call me if they have any questions. Also, please, please do not tell Peg where I am. I appreciate everything you've done for me, Miss Daisy. I'm already missing Seattle.

Yours sincerely,
Mungo Henley

The phone rang as Teddy finished and she ran out to the kitchen.

Carlo shouted. "Hurry, Teddy. We want to get started."
"Hello?"
"May I speak to Dr. Morelli, please?"
"This is she."

"Dr. Morelli, My name is Willa Sturtz. I'm a member of Derek Lee's posse?"

"Willa. Hello." How's the rat?

"Dr. Morelli, we've been meeting since Wednesday and decided we want to withdraw our protest about Louis Oliveri being Miss Asia."

"Really?"

"Yeah, we made a mistake." Willa said. "Derek didn't want us to protest anyway, and when you write down on paper why Louie shouldn't be Miss Asia, it looks really bad. All the other contestants said Louie won fair and square."

"Willa, just a moment. Do you mind repeating that?" Teddy held the phone away from her ear. "Louie, come here! Somebody wants to tell you something on the phone."

18

After dessert the boys bolted out the door to tell Louie's posse the good news. Mr. and Mrs. Oliveri lingered awhile, then made their goodbyes. Teddy showed her mother the two medications and as Marmee helped Daisy to bed, Teddy did dishes and put away food. They would get through this the same way they got through Popee's death—by merely keeping order until the day they could create something new.

She washed the gnocchi bowl, a blue and yellow Majolica with a country wedding scene. Daisy would always create something new—not only new, but delightful—and it was their job to make sure she did.

But Daisy's seed envelopes were still under the table in the living room. Teddy dried the bowl and went to the bottom of the stairs, listening, decoding sounds on the second floor. Marmee was alone in front of the bathroom mirror, putting in pincurls. The bathroom door opened and Teddy called up the stairs. "Marmee? I'm going over to see a friend. If Daisy wakes up, could you tell her I borrowed the Mercedes?"

Toiletries in hand, Marmee peeked over the banister in disbelief. After a moment she said, "Your sweater looks nice, *cara.*"

"Thanks, Marmee. Good night."

"Good night."

* * *

She had no problem with traffic: ten o'clock, Saturday night. And the Montlake Bridge was lighted at its guard-houses—elegant, idle, vaguely European. Down in the back streets of Madison Park dinner parties were just breaking up, and late-night dog walkers were pulled briskly along by animals giddy with early spring.

She parked in Aurie's front drive, uncertain that her status allowed her in back. Unloading a single box of seed envelopes from the trunk, she walked to the door and rang the bell. No one answered. There were, in fact, no lights in the house. She trotted out to the drive, checking around back. The Saab was there.

"Teddy?" Aurie called from the dark porch. He ducked quickly back inside.

She walked over, wiping her feet on the mat. She held the printing box in front of her like a birthday cake. Aurie was wearing a terry-cloth robe and his legs were bare.

"I'm sorry. You were in bed."

"No. They just got my hot tub working." He moved back to let her pass and she stepped over a puddle of water he'd left on the slate.

"I didn't mean to interrupt," she said. "You don't . . . ah . . . have company or anything, do you?"

"At this time of night?" He looked at the printing box. "What's that?"

She held it up. "The seed envelopes Daisy designed for Leo's marijuana. That's why I'm here. I have three more boxes in the trunk and I was hoping you'd let me use your shredder."

"Teddy?" He paused, baffled. "*Come* on in."

"What? What's the matter?"

"It's Saturday night! My shredder's at work."

"I know." She trotted farther down the slates. "But I wanted to get rid of the Proud Marys as soon as possible.

Could I leave them here, in case the police come by Daisy's again?''

''And why do you want to get rid of them?''

''Because Daisy could be arrested for complicity for designing marijuana envelopes.'' She carried the box back through the dark house to the kitchen and set it on the breakfast bar. From the neighbor's patio came the only light, a yellow shaft breaking over the laurel hedge.

Teddy looked out. At the end of the lawn the lake was ripply gray. Far across in Medina she could pick out the oddment of white light that was ''Gates-ville.'' Outside on the deck the hot tub burbled and hummed in the dark. Steam rose in silver billows. It was a very large tub—big enough for twelve—and Aurie had folded back the padded vinyl top, leaving half the tub still covered.

Aurie turned on the light and examined ''Proud Mary'' pasted on the printer's box. ''I didn't notice Thursday, did they find the marijuana seeds in the greenhouse?''

''I don't know. No one's called yet.''

''I've seen this picture before.''

Teddy nodded. ''It's hanging in Daisy's office.''

''I've never been to her office.'' He padded over to the bookshelves and thumbed through a stack of magazines. Pulling out a heavy booklet printed on ivory card stock, he leafed through the pages. It was the Bunny Business catalog: eightcolored, wide-spaced, trimmed with floral borders in shimmering watercolor inks. ''This really isn't my thing, but it was so beautiful I couldn't throw it away.''

''I know what you mean.'' Teddy bent down to look at the cover without disturbing him. It was last year's spring/summer issue.

''There.'' Aurie folded back the catalog. ''Isn't that the same?''

He held up the identical full-color print of Proud Mary— calico and pinafore—as on the envelopes, her lathwork name floating above.

"It is! Aurie, this is it. I bet Leo just copied it right out of the catalog. Nothing's changed at all, is it?"

"Whatever you say, dear."

"No, don't you see?" She waved the booklet. "No one could possibly say she designed new artwork for him. Knowing Leo, he probably didn't even ask."

Aurie scowled. "You didn't like him very much, did you?"

"I'd rather not think about that. It doesn't seem fair to Daisy." She placed the catalog on top of the printing box and leaned against a bar stool, trying to make out something on the other side of the lake.

"Well," he said. "I'm glad that worked out. Is that all you need?"

She darted a glance. "Actually, I've been worried about you. You haven't returned my calls."

"I don't have anything to say."

She looked him square in the face. "You're still angry, aren't you?"

"Is that what you call it?"

"I almost got you killed the other day, Aurie."

His eyes flared, he instantly mastered himself. Flatly he said, "Not just killed, nearly burned to death after a period of long anticipation." He turned away. "You will excuse me if I'm not particularly communicative."

"Aurie, you really need to deal with this."

"I know. And if you're finished, I'd like to get back in my hot tub. It's chilly out here."

"May I join you?"

Startled, he searched her face. He turned in a circle, wondering what to say. "I—I don't have any suits."

"Nor do I." Swiftly, before he could say anything, she slipped off her shoes and unlatched the porch door, tiptoeing onto the deck. The redwood planks were icy wet. In one swoop she pulled off her red sweater and tossed it onto a corner table. It was freezing cold out there.

Standing with her back to him, she slipped off her socks, bra, slacks and panties—in artful order—understanding in an instant what she had learned from all that MTV. This morning she had put on a black bra—now she saw why.

Shivering, naked as a peach, she stepped into the hot tub. The softly bubbling water was delicious. Her breasts floated, high half-globes on her chest; they reminded her of light bulbs, or Asian pears. She waited, and surged to the far side of the pool. But he might still be too angry to come out.

Inside the lights went off.

Aurie crossed the deck and stood in the dark, hands in the pockets of his terry robe. She couldn't see his face, but he stood watching her in the bubbly water.

Next door a woman on the porch strummed a rich guitar and sang. "Yesterday, all my troubles seemed so far away." She had a sweet familiar voice.

Teddy cocked her ear to the sound. "Aurie, that's Molly Thistle."

"Leo's girlfriend?"

"Whose house is that?"

Aurie sat on the edge of the tub. "Some divorced guy from the university—just moved in."

"Michael Havenaw?"

"That's right. He's the dean of academic research."

She laughed delightedly and turned on her back, searching out pale constellations in the sky.

"I need help with something here," he said.

"Certainly."

"There is, at present, a naked woman in my hot tub." He pushed his glasses up his nose. "Would you tell me if I'm reading this situation correctly?"

"Yes, Aurie. You're reading it perfectly well."

"Excellent!" He stood. "I'll be right back."

"Where are you going?"

He paused, his hand on the door latch. "They gave me a bunch of condoms at work for a joke when I divorced, but some of them look pretty interesting."

She smiled at his adorable bony legs. "Hurry back."

NOTES AND ACKNOWLEDGMENTS

At this writing the students of Seattle University have no fundraiser resembling the Miss Asia contest. This event has been fictionally transported up the interstate from the more debauched campuses of Claremont, California.

Grateful thanks to Specialty Coffee Association of America President Ted Lingle for both title and idea; Gaviña and Sons Coffee "Nose" Steve Ruiz, and Leonor Gaviña; Western Washington University botanists Susanne James and David Morgan; horticulturalists George Kaas and Joe French, Appassionato Coffee "Nose" Dan Donovan; Oncology Nutrition writer Nancy Spaulding-Albright, R.D.; Whatcom County Sheriff Detective Rod Cadman; Bellingham Police Sargeant Dave Richards; Master Locksmith Marty Casp-Detzer; Peterbilt driver Mike Wartchow; fisheries outfitter Stew Ellison; unnamed Alaska fishermen; structural engineer Preston Burris; WWU Sports Information Director Paul Madison. Geri Walker of the WWU Bureau of Faculty Research; Ian Thompson, M.D.; reader Anna Mariz; library reference staffs at Bellingham Public and Western Washington University; copy editor Eleanor Mikucki; and especially to two New York women with perfect pitch—Jane Chelius and Jennifer Sawyer Fisher.

E. J. Pugh Mysteries by
SUSAN ROGERS COOPER

"One of today's finest mystery writers"
Carolyn Hart

HOME AGAIN, HOME AGAIN
78156-5/$5.99 US/$7.99 Can

Romance author and amateur sleuth E. J. Pugh finds the latest murderous
mystery strikes much too close to home when her husband Willis disappears.

HICKORY DICKORY STALK
78155-7/$5.50 US/$7.50 Can

An invisible, high-tech prankster is wreaking havoc with E. J.'s
computer, phone lines and bank account. She suspects a creepy
neighbor kid—until he turns up dead in the Pugh family car.

ONE, TWO, WHAT DID DADDY DO?
78417-3/$5.50 US/$7.50 Can

Everyone in town is stunned by the apparent murder-suicide of the
well-liked Lester family. But E. J. may be the only one in Black
Cat Ridge who believes the murderer still walks among them.

THERE WAS A LITTLE GIRL
79468-3/$5.50 US/$7.50 Can

After saving a suicidal teenager from drowning in the river,
E.J. finds she must rescue the young girl again—this time
from a false accusation of murder.